Georgie's Heart

Kathryn Brocato

CRIMSON
ROMANCE
F+W Media, Inc.

This edition published by
Crimson Romance
an imprint of F+W Media, Inc.
10151 Carver Road, Suite 200
Blue Ash, Ohio 45242
www.crimsonromance.com

ISBN 10: 1-4405-6401-9
ISBN 13: 978-1-4405-6401-7
eISBN 10: 1-4405-6402-7
eISBN 13: 978-1-4405-6402-4

This book is dedicated to

Dr. Krishna D. Bhat

who founded the

Southeast Texas Community Health Clinic

and gave me the idea for this book

and

Mrs. Vasudha Bhat.

Chapter 1

Georgeanne Hartfield stayed at her desk and kept on working. She had hoped skipping lunch with her coworkers would buy her some peace, but she feared she was about to be proven wrong. Worse, her stomach grumbled and complained because she hadn't expected to miss her lunch today, so she hadn't brought along a sandwich.

She bent over her work as she heard the back door to the Gant Medical Clinic open. If she was lucky, they had discovered some new topic to discuss.

"Listen to this." Nurse Denise Devereaux appeared and laid the hardback book she held down flat on Georgeanne's desk with the air of one about to reveal a secret of the universe.

Georgeanne grimaced at the sight of the book her friend held so reverently. "I have work to do, Denise. I'm not getting paid to hear Fritzi Field's sexual advice."

"You aren't getting paid to miss your lunch, either," Denise returned. "Now pay attention, Georgie."

"That's telling her, Denise." Redheaded Angela Porter joined Denise in leaning over the counter in front of Georgeanne. "The rest of us would love being paid for listening to hints on improving our sex lives."

"Quiet, y'all." Sandra Whitney, a tiny blonde pixie in her starched nurse's uniform, joined the group and leaned over Denise's shoulder to study the book. "I want to hear this. Simply everyone is talking about that book."

Georgeanne gave up. She smiled upon the other three women and propped her chin on one long, shapely hand. "Go ahead, Denise. I can see I won't be able to get a thing done until you're through."

Georgeanne prayed Dr. Gant or Dr. Baghri would come in, even though she knew they were out for a long lunch. Whip-cracking doctors never came around when the clinic receptionist needed them to maintain order among the staff. The Gant Medical Clinic, which was located in the rural southeast Texas community of Fannett, usually stayed too busy for such frivolities as book readings.

Denise, the chief nurse at the Gant Clinic, drew in a deep, dramatic breath. She was a beautiful African-American woman with skin the color of milk chocolate and a figure fit for a Playboy magazine centerfold. "'If your husband makes your life miserable and blames you because you can't have an orgasm on demand, he has no right to complain if you resort to a little acting every now and then.'"

"She's got a point." Sandra leaned further over Denise's shoulder, her pale blonde hair brushing Denise's black pageboy, and peered at the book.

"Why all this uproar over a book on how to fake an orgasm?" Angela, the clinic's lab technician, wanted to know. "I don't have that sort of trouble."

Her tone implied *Why would anyone have a problem, unless she's a psych case?* Georgeanne looked thoughtfully at the tall, slender redhead.

"Neither do I," Sandra interjected, flushing. "But that doesn't mean I don't agree with Fritzi Field. Some women probably do have trouble. I mean—"

"Then they should read *The Sensuous Woman*," Angela interrupted. "Instead of wasting time learning how to fake it, they could be learning how to experience the real thing. Why all this uproar over something that's completely natural?"

Georgeanne never ceased to be amused at the rapid defensiveness of modern women when the subject of orgasm came up. Either every woman she knew experienced orgasm instantly, or every woman she knew lied. According to her friends at the Gant Clinic, sexual desire and orgasm behaved like an electrical switch. When you flipped the switch, lights turned on. Period.

"Childbirth is perfectly natural, too," Georgeanne said, "and look at all the books out on it."

"*Faking It* isn't about having an orgasm," Angela argued. "It's about faking an orgasm. There's a difference."

"Fritzi isn't talking about normal men," Denise said. "She's talking about complete jerks. I should know. I was married to one. Listen to this. 'Why let your marriage be destroyed, when it's so easy to give him what he wants?

"'Many a man thinks a woman ought not to need foreplay. He thinks she ought to be ready the minute he touches her, as if the very thought of sex with him is all that's needed. Any suggestion that this may not be the way it works sends this man into a frustrated shouting and blaming fit.

"'Who needs that?'"

The women looked at each other a moment in silent agreement when Denise finished reading that passage aloud.

"Who, indeed?" Georgeanne didn't look up from her current task of comparing a column of hand-written numbers to a copy of the column in a printed report, but she knew her cheeks glowed with telltale red her thick fall of shoulder-length brown hair might not entirely hide.

One would think that a twenty-eight-year-old woman who had been married to a man who resembled a young Robert Redford would have stopped blushing when she lost her innocence. But that wasn't the way things went with her face, Georgeanne thought with resentment. If anything, she blushed even more these days. Fritzi Field's incredible and unexpected popularity, both nationwide and inside the Gant Clinic, kept her cheeks flaming. Maybe she should claim a sunburn. Or a medical condition.

"That's what I say," Sandra declared. "A man like that deserves whatever he gets."

Angela snickered and flipped her red hair off her shoulders. "Are you kidding? He's getting a heck of a lot more than he deserves. Anyone following Fritzi Field's instructions will have the idiot thinking he's God's gift to womankind." She stretched out long, white polyester-clad legs and leaned back on Georgeanne's desk. "Fritzi Field is going around telling women to award those stupid men some sort of bad-behavior prize if you ask me. She ought to be ashamed of herself."

Georgeanne bit her full lower lip. A strange, empty feeling attacked her heart, almost as if she had stepped off a porch and found no step where one should have been.

How ridiculous. Not even she agreed with everything Fritzi Field said, so why should she feel upset when someone else didn't either?

"That isn't what Fritzi is saying—," Denise began.

Georgeanne heard with horror the respectful tone in which Denise said "Fritzi" and rushed into speech. "Fritzi Field isn't trying to say anything. She's interested in creating a controversy, because controversies sell books." She added, in a barely audible voice, "I wouldn't be surprised if Fritzi Field turns out to be a man."

"Boy, is she—or he—selling books," Denise agreed. "They're trying to line her up for all the talk shows, but her agent says she wants to remain anonymous. If I had written *Faking It*, I'd go on every single talk show that would have me."

Guilt, liberally mixed with fear, attacked Georgeanne like a battering ram to the solar plexus. She paled and stared down at the report in her hand.

Angela grinned. "Oprah Winfrey, here we come."

Denise picked through the book and opened it at another marked spot. "You're just jealous because you didn't think of writing *Faking It* first. I know I am."

Georgeanne suppressed a gasp.

"Yeah," Angela said. "You're right about that much." She folded her hands behind her frizzy red hair and gazed at the ceiling. "Do you know what I'd do if I had all that beautiful royalty money pouring into my scrawny little bank account? I'd buy myself a green Mustang convertible. That's what I'd do."

"With that red hair and pale skin of yours?" Georgeanne looked up and focused on Angela's milky, freckled skin. "You know what Dr. Gant said to you about getting in the sun ever again in your young life."

Angela ignored this comment. "I'd lose five pounds, and I'd buy a tiny black bikini with those high-cut legs, then I'd go cruising down the beach highway with the top down."

"Four walls and a roof," Georgeanne said. "That's the kind of sunscreen Dr. Gant told you to use."

"If you ever made that much money, you'd gain five pounds celebrating at the nearest bar, Angie," Denise countered. "Do you know what I'd do? I'd buy myself a lot and build a beach cabin in the ritzy section of the beach. Then I'd lose five pounds and put on my red bikini with the high-cut legs and get a tan out on my own deck."

"Yeah, Denise," Angela said, laughing. "Now that you mention it, you are looking a little pale."

"I was making a point." Denise glanced at her own dark-coffee arm with dignity. "With that kind of money, why cruise the beach in a hot car? Buy yourself a big piece of the beach."

"Not me," Sandra said in dreamy tones. "I'd buy Bobby a new car to drive to work in. His old truck is about to quit, and when it does, he'll have to use my car until we can afford a new truck."

She straightened and pushed her wispy blonde hair back beneath her nurse's cap. "What about you, Georgie? What would you do if you had big royalty checks rolling in?"

Georgeanne, cheeks flaming, looked up from her documents. She let her brown gaze drift back to the sheets of paper on her desk in a suggestive way. "You already know what I'd do with it. I'd make a big donation to Dr. Baghri's Saturday Clinic. We need more medicines—"

"Puh-leeze," Angela said. "You're such a sucker, Georgie. When Dr. Baghri talks about the poor little children, you just fall all to pieces and start volunteering. When do you have time for yourself? When do you date?"

"I don't," Georgeanne said, without rancor. She never wanted to date again. After her ex-husband had proved she wasn't woman enough to hold a man, Georgeanne figured she was better off avoiding trouble. "I'm too busy with the clinic."

"Well, the Saturday Clinic is a wonderful idea," Denise said. "But you can mark my words, it's going to fail. Charity clinics always fail because doctors hate to work for them."

"Not the way Dr. Baghri has it set up," Georgeanne said. "If he gets just forty doctors lined up, each doctor would only need to work one Saturday a year in the Clinic."

A brooding silence reigned.

Georgeanne glanced at her friends and couldn't resist a grin when she took in their serious faces. "What is it with you all? Are you trying to tell me I'm getting to be a bore on the subject of Dr. Baghri's Saturday Children's Clinic?"

The other three women chuckled and said in unison, "Who? Us?"

"Be reasonable, Georgie," Denise said. "I'll agree that Dr. Baghri's idea is brilliant. If every doctor around here who wants to do a little charity work would donate one Saturday a year, the Saturday Clinic would be a model for the rest of the United States.

The problem is getting the doctors to sign up so the Clinic can get off the ground. Right now, it's only Dr. Baghri and Dr. Gant who are carrying the load. And you."

Georgeanne had been thrilled several months before when one of the doctors she worked for had come up with a plan to help children whose parents had too much money and pride to go to the free county clinics, but not enough money to afford regular medical care. Using the Gant Clinic's facilities, Dr. Baghri had created the Saturday Children's Clinic where office visits cost only twenty dollars per visit on Saturdays.

Dr. Baghri's plan involved having each doctor in the surrounding area donate one Saturday per year of his time. The twenty-dollar charges helped offset the expenses of keeping the clinic open, and the medications were mostly free samples donated by drug companies. Community response threatened to overwhelm the clinic, thanks to local layoffs and a generally poor economy, but doctor-response so far had been less than enthusiastic.

"I'm working on that," Georgeanne said, "and so is Dr. Baghri. We'll get more doctors signed up soon. The problem is, no one quite understands how Dr. Baghri's plan works. As soon as I get my sales pitch worked out, things will be different. And I'm thinking about a web site—"

"It isn't your fault, Georgie." Denise folded her arms, book still in hand, and studied Georgeanne in a knowing way. "If that clinic fails, don't you go convincing yourself it failed because you didn't talk it up good enough."

"That's for sure." Angela pushed off Georgeanne's desk and brushed down her clinging white trousers. "You've worked as hard for the Saturday Clinic as Dr. Baghri has. Harder."

"It won't fail," Georgeanne said. "Not after Dr. Scott's widow just donated her husband's old clinic building to the cause. Which reminds me." She turned a stern gaze on her co-workers. "This weekend Dr. Baghri and I are going to be cleaning out the building and doing some painting. We're going to need a little slave labor."

Good-natured groans arose, but Georgeanne smiled with satisfaction. No matter how much her co-workers might gripe about the encroachment of the Saturday Clinic upon their free time, each and every one of them would be present for the great paint-in Georgeanne planned.

"Do you know what I wish?" Angela gave Georgeanne an affectionate grin. "I wish that just once when we talk about winning the lottery or getting big royalty checks, you'd say you're going to lose five pounds and buy a yellow bikini and a yellow convertible."

Georgeanne laughed at that. "Come on, dreamers. Five pounds won't make a dent in this body, and you know it. As for bikinis, I think I'd feel more comfortable in one of those boy-leg swimsuits."

Good-natured hooting arose. Georgeanne smiled on her friends and shook her head when they proclaimed her figure perfect as it was. A woman who stood six feet tall and who was built on a grandiose scale to boot didn't go around kidding herself about yellow bikinis. She bought a black boy-leg suit and she draped a dark towel around her overly curvaceous body.

Still, she liked knowing her friends appreciated her as she was. She certainly wasn't likely to change, not when her every effort in that direction had met with total and complete failure.

"Honey, you aren't meant to be a skinny bean pole," Denise said. "You were born with curves, and you're going to die with curves. Unless you do something stupid."

"Like get the curves liposuctioned off?" Georgeanne asked in the meek tones of one seeking information.

Denise frowned at her. "Like develop anorexia or get that weight-loss surgery. You wouldn't look right if you starved yourself down to nothing."

"Oh, give us a break." Angela walked over to gaze idly out the tall window facing Georgeanne's desk. "You're beautiful as you are, Georgie. And if you weren't so busy being soft-hearted, you'd take pity on some of the men who keep falling all over themselves trying to get you to notice them."

"What men?" Georgeanne asked. "If you're talking about poor Mr. Spector, who tripped over his little boy yesterday—"

"Brent Spector is just one of them," Denise said. "You don't see all these single fathers gazing at you when you aren't looking, but we do."

Since the Gant Clinic specialized in pediatrics, any man old enough to be gazing at Georgeanne was a father. As for men falling all over themselves to gain her notice, Georgeanne found that ridiculous.

"Let me demonstrate the way they look at you." Denise leaned forward with a sheeplike expression so full of wide-eyed longing, Georgeanne almost burst into laughter. "They're all dying to stroke those curves of yours, honey. Men think you look like a real woman."

"That's probably because I look like the motherly type. Single fathers don't need wives. They need mothers for their children." Georgeanne gathered up her papers once more.

"You don't see yourself, Georgie," Sandra said. "Men love the way you look."

Georgeanne reflected that if she had a nickel for every time she'd heard that statement or one like it, she'd be able to buy herself that yellow convertible.

"If I listened to my loyal friends, I'd be impossible to live with." She stood, papers in hand. "I'd better get these into the mail right away, or Dr. Baghri will have no one present when he dedicates the new Saturday Clinic building."

Angela pulled aside the translucent curtain and peered out the window. "Dr. Gant and Dr. Baghri just drove up. Who's that with them? Oh, my God. I'm having a heart attack." She grabbed at her chest. "Serious hottie alert, ladies." She fanned her face. "Now there's a man a woman could have an orgasm just looking at."

"Where?" Denise rushed over to join Angela at the window. "Oh, wow. He looks like a movie star. Say, I think he is a movie star. I know I've seen that face before. Isn't he the guy who played Tanner Colt in *Deuces High*?"

Sandra joined the group. "It is him. It's Hunter Howell."

"I expect it's Dr. Zane Bryant," Georgeanne said. "I've been writing him on Dr. Baghri's behalf." She went to the counter separating her cubicle from the waiting room and began folding letters and slipping them into envelopes. "Haven't you heard the story? Hunter Howell and Dr. Bryant are identical twin brothers. They were separated at birth and adopted out to different families. They found each other several years ago when Dr. Bryant saw Hunter Howell in a movie and contacted him."

"I don't care if he is just a doctor," Angela declared. "If he's coming in here, I'm going to get his autograph. He's seriously, seriously hot."

"He's coming in here." Georgeanne went back to her desk and rustled through her top drawer for stamps. "He practices pediatrics in Pasadena, and he's very interested in Dr. Baghri's idea. He wants to learn firsthand how the Saturday Clinic operates."

Pasadena was a suburb of Houston within easy driving range of Fannett. Georgeanne smiled with satisfaction, recalling the regular letters and emails she had written on Dr. Baghri's behalf to Dr. Zane Bryant over the past few weeks. She had been as thrilled as Dr. Baghri when Zane Bryant asked for an appointment to view the new clinic. The request meant her skills in coaxing reluctant doctors into donating time to charity showed improvement.

"Oh, please," Angela groaned. "Don't tell me all he's going to be talking about is charity clinics. What a waste."

"You don't mean that," Georgeanne said with gentle reproof. "You were the first person to volunteer when Dr. Baghri couldn't get a lab tech for the Saturday Clinic."

"Well, tell the world, why don't you?" Angela stared out the window. "If a woman was married to a man who looked like that, she wouldn't need Fritzi Field's advice on how to fake it."

Georgeanne's face flamed, and she wished for the millionth time that she wouldn't blush every time anyone mentioned Fritzi Field. One of her friends might draw the correct conclusion any day now: Georgeanne Hartfield had a guilty conscience.

Two years ago, Georgeanne's handsome husband left her for another woman. During the period immediately after her divorce, Georgeanne had produced a book. The writing had assuaged her anguish and helped her come to terms with her dead marriage.

The book had blessed her in more ways than one. It had been excellent psychological therapy, and the money from its sale helped finance Dr. Baghri's clinic and bought dog food for the Humane Society, among other things.

Georgeanne simply hadn't expected the book to take off the way it had, much less that it would be waved in her face every day at work.

Lord help her if anyone ever realized Georgeanne Hartfield was the reclusive, controversial author, Fritzi Field. Everyone would know she had lost her husband because she was lacking as a woman, and Georgeanne didn't think she could stand that.

The group at the window scattered. Angela hustled back to her lab and the two nurses scurried off in opposite directions.

Georgeanne remained at her post, pasting stamps on the envelopes she had already addressed. She would get a close-up view of Dr. Zane Bryant soon enough. Besides, a woman who had been married to a man who resembled Robert Redford knew better than to let a man's good looks sway her common sense.

The front door opened and three men entered. One assumed an instant prone position on the floor when a blue toy car flew from beneath his foot and bounced off the wall.

"Dr. Bryant!" Aghast, Georgeanne rushed through the swinging door that separated her from the waiting area and knelt beside him while Dr. Gant and Dr. Baghri gazed down in paralyzed horror. "Are you all right? Oh, this is all my fault. I didn't see that car when I straightened the office this morning. I'm so very sorry."

"It's not your fault, Georgie," Dr. Gant, a tall, thin man with graying hair said in stunned tones. "Cleaning the office isn't your job in the first place."

Georgeanne winced. That meant the clinic's regular cleaning woman, who was at home nursing her sick mother at Georgeanne's insistence, might be in trouble. If only she could learn to think before she spoke.

"My apologies, doctor." Vijay Baghri, a short Indian man, joined Georgeanne in kneeling beside Zane Bryant's prone figure, and his small dark hands joined Georgeanne's efforts in assisting Dr. Bryant. "Dr. Gant will perhaps hire a new cleaning person."

"Not on my account, please," Dr. Bryant said. "The truth is, I was born clumsy."

Georgeanne gave a sigh of relief. There lay a rare man indeed, a young good-looking doctor who wasn't so stuck on himself, he sought revenge on anyone who placed him in a ridiculous position.

"It was my fault," she said in firm, no-nonsense tones. "That truck wasn't there this morning when we opened, or I'd have been the one on the floor. Here, Dr. Bryant. Let me—"

Then Georgeanne met the fallen doctor's gaze and found herself as breathless as if she had taken the fall herself.

Laid out full-length on Dr. Gant's blue carpet, his black hair disarranged by the fall and tumbled across his forehead, Dr. Bryant lay perfectly still and stared up at her. The way his smoky, gray eyes focused on her in such a dazed fashion, she feared a concussion.

Oh, he was a stunningly handsome man all right, but handsome men were as litigious as ugly men, especially when an incident involved damage to their self-image.

He kept staring at her, and Georgeanne felt the full focus of his attention with an unprecedented, purely feminine sensation she found almost as disturbing as her fears of concussion.

She took herself in hand. Dr. Bryant had come to learn about Dr. Baghri's Saturday Clinic. Her job was to promote the clinic with every fiber of her being. Nothing else mattered.

• • •

Zane Bryant rolled over and looked up from his nose-down position on the floor. He found himself face-to-face with a goddess. Or an angel. He wondered if more than the breath had been knocked out of him by the unexpected fall.

She was almost as tall as he was, and she had soft, candid, dark-brown eyes framed with incredibly long, curling lashes that reminded him of a doe's eyes. She had skin like that of a porcelain doll, all pink and white, and full red lips that needed no lipstick.

Moreover, she was soft with lush feminine curves, and the hands that supported his shoulders were long and strong and slender, the hands of a woman who wasn't afraid of work. She looked like a woman who valued people more than she valued intangibles. Or a career, he added in his mind.

In spite of many self-lectures about the folly of imagining virtues into a woman just because of the letters and emails she wrote, Zane knew he was guilty of exactly that.

He didn't really know her yet, he reminded himself. That's why he was here.

Zane came to himself at last and realized he still lay on the floor like an idiot. He let them assist him to a sitting position and tried to gather his wits.

"Miss Hartfield?" he wheezed. Damn, but he'd taken quite a fall. He wished he wasn't so clumsy. Talk about making a miserable first impression on a beautiful woman.

She smiled and looked relieved. "Yes, I'm Georgeanne Hartfield. This isn't the way we wanted to welcome you, Doctor."

"I can assure you, I'll never forget my first sight of you." Zane smiled and placed one hand over his heart while he remained seated on the floor. She smelled of lilies. Zane decided lilies were his favorite flowers. "Keep your cleaning woman, Dr. Gant. She just did me a great favor."

Georgeanne laughed. Zane considered the warm glow of gratitude in those gorgeous brown eyes an unexpected reward.

"The doctor does not need our help to get himself to his feet," Dr. Baghri said in his humorous, broken English. "Our Georgie will lift him up by his heart."

Georgeanne blushed. "Hush, Doctor. You'll have our guest thinking I do heart transplants on the side."

Zane Bryant stared again in spite of his fear that Georgeanne might consider him rude. This magnificent creature actually blushed. If she was the Georgeanne Hartfield who had been corresponding with him on Vijay Baghri's behalf for the past few weeks, his good fortune looked too incredible to be true.

He rolled to his feet and reached down to help Georgeanne up. She stood only a few inches shorter than he did.

Splendid, he thought.

He wasn't aware that he still held her hand and gazed at her face until Dr. James Gant cleared his throat in a meaningful way.

"Thank you, Dr. Bryant." Georgeanne withdrew her hand with a startled look. "I'd better get back to work. Dr. Baghri's letters are almost ready to go out. We're dedicating the new clinic location in a couple of weeks."

"I hope I'm invited," Zane said.

Georgeanne gave him a swift, impersonal smile. "Of course you're invited. If you'll stop by my desk on your way out, I'll see to it that you get your invitation this afternoon."

Zane wondered if he could get out of touring the Saturday Clinic so he could get to know Georgeanne. Or better, if he could talk Georgeanne into acting as his tour-guide.

Georgeanne directed another smile in his direction and hurried back to her desk where the telephone sounded an insistent appeal.

While Zane pretended to listen to Dr. Baghri's discourse, he noted that Georgeanne apparently reached the phone too late, because it stopped ringing. She looked at it in a regretful way and reached for some papers on her desk.

A dignified black woman in a white nurse's uniform appeared at the counter behind Georgeanne's desk. Georgeanne looked up with a warm smile. Zane wished she would direct all her smiles at him.

"Who was on the phone?" he heard Georgeanne ask.

"Mrs. Miguez is holding for Dr. Baghri," the black woman said. "Tammy's asthma is acting up again, and she's panicking."

"Oh, dear." Georgeanne looked distressed and stood at once. "Dr. Baghri says she may have to be hospitalized this time. I'd better put him on immediately."

"Have you seen my copy of *Faking It?*" the nurse asked. "I thought—there it is. You put your papers on top of it."

Georgeanne glanced at the book on her desk and turned scarlet. Zane searched his memory but couldn't immediately place the title. He resolved to look into the matter further. Anything that caused this incredible woman to blush interested him.

"What is it with you?" the nurse asked. "Every time I so much as mention this book, you do an imitation of a boiled lobster."

"We have a visitor," Georgeanne said, almost choking. "Would you mind getting that silly book off my desk?"

"What for?" the nurse asked, grinning. "Are you afraid the visiting doctor might see it and make a few assumptions?"

Georgeanne ignored that and hurried out of her office cubicle. She approached the doctors and spoke a few sentences in Dr. Baghri's ear.

Zane watched her approach, smiled at her, and wished she would come close enough to speak in his ear. To his intense interest, she returned his smile and hurried back to her desk.

The telephone rang, and Georgeanne answered it without looking up when Zane crossed the room and glanced around her small cubicle.

"Yes, Mrs. St. George," she said. "Yes, that's the one. Thank you for telling me."

Zane watched the smile that crept over her face with deep interest. She laughed, and Zane found himself equally fascinated by her full, rich chuckle.

"The article is based on my observations from working in a children's clinic for several years," she went on. "I'm so glad you enjoyed it." She listened a moment. "Well, someday I hope to have children of my own, of course. One of these days, when Mr. Right comes along."

Zane's mind filled in the other side of the conversation. Georgeanne had written an article. That didn't surprise him at all, considering the way he'd been pouncing on her epistles for the past few weeks.

What did surprise him was the image that rose in his mind of Georgeanne with a dark-headed baby at her breast. In his years as a pediatrician, he had seen many, many women with babies at their breasts, but none of those real images rocked him the way the vision of Georgeanne did.

All he had to do to make it come true was convince Georgeanne she had at last met Mr. Right.

Chapter 2

Zane couldn't believe his luck. He hadn't needed to say a word, and here he sat in Georgeanne Hartfield's red SUV. They headed for the building that would become the new Saturday Clinic, while Dr. Vijay Baghri drove to a hospital in nearby Beaumont where little Tammy Miguez was being admitted.

Better yet, Georgeanne had discarded the white linen jacket she wore in the clinic. Only a clingy calf-length yellow jersey dress covered her satin skin. He admired the lush feminine curves beneath the yellow jersey and tried in a half-hearted way to keep his imagination under some semblance of control. He'd only met the lady an hour ago, and already he imagined what she looked like in the nude.

He thanked the heavens that Georgeanne Hartfield showed no signs of either doctor reverence or celebrity worship, nor did she quiz him about his famous brother. The only thing on her mind appeared to be explaining Dr. Baghri's Saturday clinic so that he would understand the brilliance of the idea.

Zane wondered how long it would take him to become the primary item on Georgeanne Hartfield's mind.

"Sorry about the grand entrance." He ignored the spreading green rice fields and stands of spring-green Chinese tallow trees that surrounded them in favor of gazing at Georgeanne's magnificent fall of brown hair and her porcelain complexion. "I've never learned to pick up my feet."

"It wasn't your fault." Georgeanne turned down the vehicle down a narrow dirt road that ran between two newly cultivated rice fields. "I simply didn't look at the floor the way I should have when I straightened the office earlier."

"It wasn't exactly the sort of entrance guaranteed to impress a woman," he said.

"Oh, I don't think you need to worry about first impressions." She gave him a merry smile. "I was the only woman present in the office when you came in."

She had no idea, Zane realized with some astonishment, no idea at all that she was the only woman whose first impression counted with him. He found it both refreshing and annoying.

"You're saying then, that your image of me as a debonair, well-coordinated individual wasn't totally destroyed by that pratfall?" he asked.

Georgeanne's warm, dark chocolate eyes twinkled. "Doctor, I am forever grateful to you for claiming it was your own clumsiness rather than my carelessness that caused the unfortunate incident."

"I'm happy to have been of service," he said. "I suppose what you're not saying is that you were picking up the office because your cleaning woman is off with a sick headache or something."

Georgeanne laughed, a throaty laugh of real amusement. "You're very nearly right, but please don't say anything to the doctors. Our cleaning woman can't afford to lose this job. Her mother is quite ill and needs constant care."

The spring sunlight gleamed off Georgeanne's hair. Zane thought he had never seen hair so thick, or of such a rich and deep brown. He wanted to thrust his fingers into that hair and glove both his hands in it.

"I was sure it must be something like that." She had a beautiful profile as well as the kind heart he'd suspected.

She turned the steering wheel, and his gaze fastened upon the motions of her graceful hands. He could watch those hands all day, he decided. He'd like most of all to watch them spread heat and comfort across his prone body after a hard day of examining small patients.

"I've temporarily hidden all the blue toys that blend into the carpet." Georgeanne gave her delicious chuckle and turned the SUV into a rutted, overgrown, shell-covered parking lot before a single-story brick building with boarded-up windows. "This is our new building. Dr. Baghri received the deed from Mrs. Scott day before yesterday. Isn't it wonderful?"

Zane looked, well aware that he was probably one of the few people who truly thought it wonderful. Only die-hards like himself and Georgeanne Hartfield could see anything wonderful about the neglected brick building surrounded by a grove of fast-growing tallow trees, out in the middle of nowhere.

"I've been impressed with the progress you've reported in establishing the Saturday Children's Clinic," Zane said. "Are you sure people will come all the way out here?"

"They came from all over the area when old Dr. Scott was alive," she said. "If they came for Dr. Scott, they'll come for the Saturday Children's Clinic."

She parked the Cherokee and didn't wait for Zane to leap out and come around for her. By the time he got his feet on the ground, she applied a key to the door of the boarded-up building.

Zane watched her, thinking hard. The lady obviously wasn't used to receiving common courtesies from men. Zane intended to remedy that before she grew much older.

"Dr. Baghri and I were here yesterday evening assessing what needs to be done," Georgeanne said. "Dr. Scott died three years ago, and the building has been empty ever since." She shoved open the door and stepped inside without hesitation. "The first thing we're going to have to do is apply a little old-fashioned elbow grease and give it a thorough cleaning."

Zane followed and cast a swift glance around. The clinic was a bare shell without furniture. The walls were discolored with mildew, the paint was peeling, and the electricity had long ago been cut off. The musty odor of mildew overrode the fresh spring scents of plowed ground and honeysuckle outside. The forlorn, neglected appearance of the place would have frightened most women into refusing to set foot inside.

But not Georgeanne.

"You mean you're going to give it a thorough cleaning." Zane felt sure he knew Georgeanne well enough to guess at that.

"I'll have help," Georgeanne said.

Sure you will, Zane thought. He sniffed and detected the faint odor of lilies on the mildew-scented air.

"I've got lots of people lined up." She flicked on a flashlight and played it over the linoleum floor. Debris covered the floor, everything from empty paper cups to old magazines. "The utility company is sending someone out to restore the electrical service this afternoon. Once we have light, we can start cleaning. Dr. Baghri has already ordered the new phone system, and it'll be installed Monday. That means we have the weekend to get the place cleaned and painted."

"That's a true volunteer's 'we'," Zane said, amused and annoyed at the same time. "You're the one who's going to be doing most of the work."

Georgeanne chuckled again, and the sparkling laughter moved something inside his heart. "You may have a point there. I enjoy cleaning, so I'll probably do most of it myself during the next two days. Normal people enjoy painting, so I'm saving my volunteers for the big paint-in Saturday."

"You're not a normal person?" Zane asked.

Georgeanne tossed her heavy mane of hair off her shoulders and looked around the moldy room in a possessive way. "I think everyone who knows me would probably agree that I'm not."

"Because you like to clean rather than paint?" He stared at her mouth. Even in the dim light, he could see her soft, full lips.

"That's as good a reason as any, don't you think?" She turned dark-brown eyes on him that invited him to laugh with her.

Zane laughed and decided he needed to help in the preparations to open the Saturday Clinic. He thanked heaven that he wasn't on call that weekend.

"There are two examining rooms." Georgeanne stepped carefully across a mound of debris. Cockroaches scattered at her approach, but she ignored them. "Dr. Baghri's chief worry when we hosted the Clinic in our office was that the volunteer doctors might refuse to examine patients in somebody else's office. That's why we're so overjoyed about receiving this building."

"I understand." Zane followed behind her.

"If I can make volunteering here sound like an adventure, I'll bet we get more doctors than we need."

Zane agreed, enjoying the nuances in Georgeanne's voice as much as he liked her words.

She meant it. Although the clinic was officially Dr. Baghri's idea, it was Georgeanne's faithful execution that ensured the clinic's success. He recalled how diligently she'd corresponded with him on Dr. Baghri's behalf, just to get him to donate a Saturday or two of his time during the year.

"This is where the clinic's lab used to be." Georgeanne shined the light over a dark, dank room furnished only with a long filthy counter and a double sink. "I'm sure the plumbing is still in good condition, but just in case, I'll call a plumber friend of mine out Monday to check things over."

"Do you have friends in almost every profession?" he asked.

She must have heard the amusement in his voice because she turned toward him with eagerness. "Just about. No electricians, though." He sensed the humorous hope in her. "Maybe you know someone you can introduce me to?"

"Sorry." He laughed with her. "I can see I've been remiss. All this time, I should have been making friends in high places."

"It isn't too late to begin." She redirected the light beam so he could see to exit the room.

Zane stepped carefully over some debris and examined the sink. "I've wanted to be part of something like this ever since I started practice. When a friend told me of Dr. Baghri's Saturday Clinic for children, I knew I needed to check it out."

"We're very glad you did," Georgeanne said. "We're just beginning, and at this point, every doctor counts. Plus, the more doctors who participate, the more doctors will want to join us."

Zane intended to examine every square inch of the unprepossessing building and prolong his time alone with Georgeanne. He could listen to her rich, cheerful voice all day. "Dr. Baghri is lucky to have you on his side. His English isn't the best at times."

"That's why he started out by recruiting me." Georgeanne laughed. "He claims I'm his official spokesperson when it comes to the Clinic."

"He couldn't have chosen anyone better," Zane said with feeling.

He directed his thoughts toward methods of spending more time with Georgeanne Hartfield and wondered how long it would take her to realize his interest in the Saturday Clinic took a back seat to his interest in her.

• • •

Georgeanne led the way back out to the parking lot, where the bright spring sunshine cast a glow over the neglected building. Glancing up at Zane, she registered once more how tall he was, but she refused to let herself dwell on the fleeting thought that he was among the few men who were taller than she was. Nor did she allow herself to entertain the thought that his dark hair called for feminine fingers to fork it into order. She refused to consciously notice the thick, dark lashes that framed those incredible smoky eyes, or the slashing black brows above them.

Looks were not important in this case, she told herself. Compassion for sick children counted for everything.

And Dr. Baghri depended on her to explain his idea to other doctors and gain more volunteers to help those sick children.

"Dr. Baghri has been treating lots of children in the hospital emergency room during the past few years," she began, "simply because they were too poor to see a family physician for routine medical care. When a child finally got so sick he had to see a doctor, the parents had no choice but to bring him to the emergency room because they didn't have a family doctor."

"I've seen a lot of that myself," Zane said in grim tones. "When it comes to a choice between regular medical checkups or eating, parents nearly always choose eating."

He took Georgeanne's arm and walked her around the side of the building. His action surprised her and she ignored the speedier beat of her heart. Half the physicians in Southeast Texas probably ran when they saw her coming because of Dr. Baghri's efforts to push her charms before his colleagues.

Georgeanne felt her pulse accelerate a bit more and told herself not to be a fool. She'd known Zane Bryant would resemble the handsome Hunter Howell. She just hadn't allowed for the man's sheer physical impact on her impressionable senses.

Why a fairly young doctor like Zane Bryant wanted to spend his rare leisure time examining a charity clinic in her company when he could be sailing or playing golf was not for her to question. She—and Dr. Baghri—needed him.

Dr. Bryant, she told herself, might be the doctor who would turn the tide in her struggle to recruit doctors for the clinic. She ignored the feminine jitters his presence provoked and strove to remember her talking points.

"Dr. Baghri remembered his own year of practice in India before he came to America," Georgeanne went on. "When he graduated from medical school he went home to his own little village in India, rented a single room, and screened off an examining room with bed sheets. He charged the poor people a small fee, and the rich people a larger fee, and everyone got the same consideration from the doctor. So he thought, why couldn't he do this in America?"

She felt Zane squeeze her arm, and then his fingers cupped around her elbow. His warm, supportive grip gave her an unaccustomed feeling that she was protected and cared for.

"But in America, it was not easy to do that," Georgeanne went on. "In America, you either pay a set price, or you pay nothing at county charity clinics. There are no allowances for differences in income."

"In America," Zane said in dry tones, "the doctor usually doesn't know which patients are rich and which are poor. During my residency, I treated a few millionaires I thought were bums and some bums who dressed like millionaires."

"Exactly," Georgeanne said, pleased with his ready understanding. "In America, free clinics exist for poor people, but the workers are so overwhelmed with the problems of the poor, they often fail to treat the patients with compassion. What's more, the fact that the clinics are free robs the patients of what little dignity they have left. So Dr. Baghri came up with the idea of charging everyone twenty dollars. Even poor people can usually afford twenty dollars."

Georgeanne made this point with great earnestness, punctuating it with a sweeping gesture of one of her graceful hands. Her hand struck the trunk of an encroaching tallow tree.

"Ouch," she exclaimed and jerked her hand back. "That's another little item I'll have to see to—tree removal."

Zane reached for Georgeanne's injured hand and examined the reddened area. "It just so happens that I worked as a tree removal apprentice one summer during my youth."

"You did?"

Conscious of a peculiar, winded feeling, Georgeanne stood there and let him study the minuscule scratches on the edge of her hand. His hands were big and blunt, but possessed the deft gentleness she had come to expect of physicians' hands. Her hand looked small and delicate sandwiched between Zane's, an unusual event for Georgeanne.

He looked up and smiled at her. "Of course it was a good fifteen years ago, but I still remember all the rope tricks necessary to cutting a tree down limb by limb without damaging the building beneath it." Zane turned her hand over and examined the strong lines marking her palm. "Now there's a life line to be proud of."

Georgeanne's breath wheezed out. Her heart pounded so furiously, she could hardly speak. How silly, letting herself get all worked up because a good-looking man held her hand.

"You're a palm reader, too?" she asked in choked tones.

"It doesn't take any training to recognize a hand filled with promises of long life and love." He lifted her palm and kissed the center. "A palm like this is a rare find indeed."

Georgeanne stood stock still a moment, staring down at her own palm. She felt hot and cold all over, and her heart fluttered with a beat quite unlike its usual calm rhythm. Perhaps, she thought, with wry humor, she ought to see a doctor.

Recovering herself with a jolt, Georgeanne looked up and laughed. "What you mean is this palm would be very welcome at certain upcoming events in Houston, especially where cleaning skills are needed."

"Miss Hartfield—Georgeanne—you have a palm that would be welcome anywhere, cleaning skills or no."

Georgeanne sighed with relief. She had managed to extricate herself from that one without making a total fool of herself. She needed to get herself—and him—back to the office before she did something really stupid, like twist her ankle.

Rather than suggest an immediate return to the Gant Clinic, Georgeanne dwelled with considerable pleasure on what Zane Bryant's large strong hands would feel like on her ankle. She progressed from there to imagining herself riding high in his arms as he carried her back to her car. Worse, he held on to her hand, which added fuel to the fantasy.

Zane bent his arm and slipped her hand into the crook of his elbow. Then he walked her slowly around the building, pointing out the tallow trees that ought to go. Georgeanne concentrated on not tripping over any of the debris in her way and refused to let herself clutch his arm.

"Am I making you nervous?" he asked and glanced down at her hand. "How can you possibly be nervous of a man who first greeted you from a prone position on the floor?"

"Me? Nervous?" Georgeanne prided herself on her lack of nerves. "I'm just thinking about everything that needs to be done in the next week or two. What do you think about these three trees that have sprung up against the building?"

"They have to go, or they'll interfere with the building's foundation." Zane paused to study the three slender tallow trees.

"When the excess trees are cleared away, this will be a peaceful country clinic once again." Georgeanne felt enthusiasm bubble inside her as she gazed on the site, and thought of the culmination of her work. "I can't wait to get started on the cleaning and painting."

Zane looked at her in such a peculiar way, she wondered what she'd said to bring on that expression.

"Neither can I," he said.

• • •

"Georgie, you make big splash with Dr. Bryant," Dr. Vijay Baghri called from the door of the old Scott Clinic building. "He will help with this clinic all the way."

Georgeanne smiled, pleased. She stood in the center of the floor in the old laboratory, rake in hand, and called back, "He's a very nice man. He says he knows how to saw down trees." She laughed and added, "He shouldn't have told me that."

"Because you will put him to work?" Dr. Baghri's head appeared around the corner of the door. "But Georgie, he wants you to put him to work. He says he will work all day, any day for you." The doctor gestured at something behind him. "We will soon have plenty of doctors to help us."

Dr. Bryant appeared behind Dr. Baghri. He hadn't gone back to Pasadena after all. Georgeanne's eyes widened, and she knew a moment of panic. Of all the times to be wearing her oldest, baggiest jeans and a T-shirt that had been accidentally washed with bleach.

Then she remembered that she had no business thinking she could attract a man who probably had every society beauty in Houston chasing him. She wanted to get this clinic ready to open as fast as possible. If Dr. Zane Bryant was willing to work, then she had plenty of work for him to do.

"Hello, Georgie." Zane adopted the friendly diminutive everyone addressed her by. "Are you out here all alone?"

The austere tone he used let her know that fact displeased him. Georgeanne gripped her rake as she assimilated that and wondered what he meant by it. Everyone knew she preferred to do certain jobs alone.

"I just got here," she said. "I thought it would be a good idea to get the floors raked before the real cleaning starts. Hi, Raza." She nodded at Dr. Baghri's wife, who carried a broom and a mop. "In another few minutes, I'll have the floor cleared of all this junk."

"In the future, don't come out here until Dr. Baghri or Dr. Gant arrives," Zane said sternly. "You're out here in the middle of a rice field, with no telephone service and no way to get help if something should happen."

"I have my cell phone in my purse." Georgeanne raked trash into a huge pile. "And I knew Dr. Baghri and Raza were due at any minute. In fact, I was hoping to be through raking before they got here."

"In the future, don't do it," Zane said, in stern tones. "Vijay, I want you to see to it that she isn't out here by herself anymore."

Dr. Baghri said something to the effect that Georgeanne operated on her own timetable and always got things done with efficiency. To Georgeanne's astonishment, Zane interrupted with a passionate discourse on a man's responsibility to look out for a woman's safety. She and Raza Baghri exchanged amused glances.

For a moment, Georgeanne thought about pointing out that she was not the sort of woman who required manly protection. She thought better of it. Zane Bryant thought she did, and who was she to argue?

Dr. Baghri gave in. "I will see to it. Georgeanne shall not work here alone any longer."

"See that she doesn't." Zane looked satisfied, although he grinned when he caught the expression on Georgeanne's normally serene countenance. "Too bad, Georgie. I know you intend to do exactly as you please. Just so you know, I'm prepared to enforce my dictates."

Georgeanne noted the expression of anticipation on his face and wondered how he planned to obtain her obedience. For a brief moment, her spirit rose to the challenge and she considered finding out.

Zane waded through the trash on the floor and held out his hand. "Here, Georgie. Give me that rake. You can start sweeping off the counter."

Georgeanne realized she stood in the presence of a man who intended to see she didn't strain herself. The idea stunned her into unaccustomed meekness. She handed him the rake and went to fetch a whisk broom from the boxes she carted in her vehicle.

"Now I see why you own an SUV." Zane raked with vigor. "You use it to haul cleaning supplies around."

"I do tend to do a lot of hauling." Georgeanne found herself in what amounted to an alternate universe.

"That's what I figured." He sounded satisfied.

She whisked off the counter in silence and pondered the meaning of that remark, then glanced over her shoulder. Zane raked a large pile of trash through the door to the outside with great energy. She let her eyes dwell with pleasure on his broad shoulders and his well-shaped backside.

He had changed into khaki trousers and a madras plaid shirt, and Georgeanne thought he looked twice as handsome in casual clothing. But that was because the blue plaid shirt made his eyes look blue, she decided. Or maybe the dingy walls that caused the newly restored electrical lights to cast a less powerful glow were what darkened his eyes to blue.

It was no business of hers what color his eyes were.

Georgeanne whisked at the counter with renewed vigor and wondered what color those eyes would be if she could see them really close up. Say, within six inches of her face.

What a delicious fantasy. It almost banished from her distracted mind the phone call that had awaited her when she arrived home from work that afternoon.

Fritzi Field was so much in demand that Alice Anson, Georgeanne's agent, claimed a pending nervous breakdown from having to turn down so much money.

"So put on a wig, kid. No one will know it's you. Think of the commission I could be making. Think of the publicity. Think of the money you could be making."

"Bear up, Alice." Georgeanne felt like a wicked agent-torturer. "If the fans can't hear what Fritzi has to say, maybe they'll fork over more money and buy their own copy of her book so they can read what she says."

Alice groaned. "You're ruining my bank account, Georgie."

Georgeanne felt cruel, although reasonably satisfied. Alice would never jeopardize their relationship by revealing Georgeanne's identity. But according to Alice, an enterprising investigator would uncover the truth eventually, no matter what steps Georgeanne took to remain anonymous.

Not, Georgeanne thought, an uplifting view of the future.

She gulped and wondered once more what had possessed her to write that book. She must have been a lot more devastated by her late, great marriage than she'd let herself believe.

Maybe she ought to go ahead and reveal her identity.

Georgeanne let herself contemplate that for about one second before a shiver of horror swept through her. She hated being in the limelight, especially when she thought about revealing the intimate details of her former marriage. Imagine having everyone know she hadn't been woman enough to keep her husband. As for facing talk show hosts full of intimate questions, she couldn't even bring herself to contemplate it.

Thoughts of curious talk show hosts added extra energy to Georgeanne's whisk broom, almost as much as fantasizing about the color of Zane Bryant's eyes.

When the entire clinic floor had been raked and swept, Georgeanne marshaled her small crew into order and passed out stepladders, scrub buckets, sponges, and brushes. While Vijay and Raza Baghri started on the big waiting room, Georgeanne began on the laboratory and assigned Zane one of the examining rooms.

"Do you store all this equipment yourself?" Zane asked in belligerent tones. "It's obvious you're used to directing cleaning crews. You've got everything down to a fine art."

Georgeanne, balanced upon a stepladder with a brush in her hand and a bucket of hot water liberally laced with cleaner sitting on the ladder's platform, laughed down at him. He stood in the center of the old laboratory with both fists planted on his lean hips. His smoky eyes were dark with concern, as if he feared she would fall off the ladder, she realized, astonished.

"I'm friends with the owner of a rent-all store," she said. "He advises me about what I need for different jobs."

"Now I see why you bought a four-wheel-drive with a roomy back end," Zane said. "Do you do this every weekend?"

"Heavens, no. If I did, I'd quit my job and open a professional cleaning service." Georgeanne dipped her brush into the lemon-scented water and applied it vigorously to a patch of mildew on the ceiling.

Zane dodged aside as water flew in all directions. "I want to know one thing, Georgie. What do you do for relaxation?"

Georgeanne laughed. "My idea of relaxation is a good book and a fresh cup of coffee. Why do you think I'm so easy-going and even-tempered?"

"Is that what you are?" Zane moved a little further away. "I thought I was working for one of those guys on a slave ship who walks up and down with a whip."

As Georgeanne knew her cleaning style tended to be vigorous and involved lots of water, she couldn't blame him for keeping his distance.

She dipped her brush in the water again. "I'm a sweet-tempered, laid-back person. Everyone says so."

"Is that right? When does a laid-back person such as yourself take a break?"

Georgeanne checked her watch. "In exactly one hour."

"You'll stop now. You've been going like a steam engine for over two hours. The doctor has spoken."

Georgeanne's brush never paused. "Doctor, it's time you learned something."

Zane advanced to the center of the room once more. "Call me Zane. What is it I'm to learn?"

"When I'm outside the office, I have no respect for medical degrees." She leaned over her bucket and smiled at him. "In case you haven't noticed, I'm running the show around here. In short, I'm the boss."

He stared up at her. "Are you trying to tell me something that might be disastrous to my medical ego?"

"That's right." She dipped her brush once more. "Until this clinic is open, everyone in here, doctors included, does what I say, and I say I am not taking a break for another hour."

Zane retreated when she reapplied the brush to the ceiling. "What you need is a lesson in how to treat a doctor with delicate sensibilities."

That surprised a laugh out of her. "That will probably require more work than you care to undertake, Doctor."

Zane's voice held enough silky threat to speed Georgeanne's heart up once more.

"Don't bet on it," he said. "It's going to give me great pleasure to be your instructor, Georgie Hartfield."

Chapter 3

"Wait till you hear this," Denise said.

"I do not want to hear it, Denise." Georgeanne set another envelope into her printer and tapped out an address on the keyboard. "I have my regular work to do plus addressing these announcements for Dr. Baghri's press conference."

Denise ignored this. She strolled into Georgeanne's small office with her fingers marking a place in Fritzi Field's book. "This sounds just like something you'd say, Georgie."

Georgeanne's blood ran cold. The telephone erupted and she pounced on it with relief, then buzzed Dr. Gant's office.

It was Friday, and Georgeanne had finally finished the major scrub-work on the new clinic building late the night before. Thinking about tonight made her heart beat faster, and she couldn't kid herself that her excitement stemmed from the fact that the clinic was almost ready for next weekend's opening ceremony. She knew she hoped to see Zane Bryant, who had promised to come to Fannett that weekend and help with the painting.

Denise waited, fingertip on the relevant passage. "All right, Georgie. The sooner you listen, the sooner I'll cease and desist." She grinned. "I know you'd rather sit there and daydream about that handsome hunk Dr. Bryant, but look at it this way. Fritzi Field might have some advice you can use."

"Denise..." Georgeanne gave up. Her co-workers claimed Dr. Zane Bryant looked at her the way he'd look at a choice *hors d'oeuvre*. Georgeanne considered that unlikely, but wonderfully exciting to think about all the same. "All right. Go ahead."

Denise cleared her throat and held the book out like an actor declaiming a monologue.

"'Once a woman has chosen acting as a profession within her marriage, she can never turn back. If you are wise, you will edit your brain cells so that when you are angry, the truth will not spill out. In short, if you decide you're justified in faking it, don't think you can yell the truth at him every time you get mad and your marriage will survive.

"'Nothing infuriates a man more, or destroys his trust more surely than discovering his wife has lied to him about a matter so intimately connected with his ego.

"'Ladies, let me assure you of one thing. If you get nothing else out of this book, get this: *If you decide to fake orgasm, you'd better plan to keep on faking it, because this is a case wherein honesty will NEVER be the best policy.*'"

Georgeanne recalled the passage well. She had underlined it, set it off in italics, and bolded that passage in a way she hoped would call a reader's attention to the seriousness of the idea expressed.

She cultivated her face into an expression of mild interest in spite of the color she knew flared in her cheeks. "Well, I'd say Fritzi Field has stated the case with exactitude. That's one point I wouldn't dream of arguing with."

Denise looked over the top of the book at Georgeanne in a searching way.

"When you get through with that book, Denise, may I borrow it?" Sandra asked.

Georgeanne turned with gratitude. The small blonde leaned over the back counter, listening in apparent fascination.

"Dare we ask why you want to borrow it?" Angela asked in teasing tones. She joined Sandra in leaning against the back counter.

The three women had just returned from lunch, a lunch Georgeanne had declined on the excuse of addressing those press notices. Georgeanne realized with some horror that Denise had improved the lunch by reading aloud educational passages from *Faking It*.

"I'm interested in what else she has to say," Sandra said. "Fritzi Field is probably going to save a lot of marriages."

"That's what I think," Denise said. "Do you know what's weird?"

Too suffocated to reply, Georgeanne fastened all her attention on the envelope she had just laid in her printer and hoped her hair screened her face. Thank goodness her natural modesty had kept her from showing her colleagues her published magazine articles. They thought she wrote a few things here and there as a hobby—if they remembered she wrote. She sincerely hoped they didn't remember she wrote.

"What?" Angela asked. "Other than Fritzi Field's screwball method of saving marriages, I mean."

"When I read that passage, I can almost hear Georgie talking," Denise said.

The bottom dropped out of Georgeanne's stomach. Everything in front of her eyes went momentarily dark.

"You're right." Sandra tapped the counter in agreement. "Georgie sounds exactly the same way when she's trying to make a point. One minute she sounds like a doctor, and the next minute she sounds like your mother."

Georgeanne smothered a soft moan and prayed for strength. When she had finished writing *Faking It* and submitted it to an agent, she'd honestly thought that if the book got published, it might make her a tidy little advance she could donate to the Humane Society. She never thought to see so much as a single copy of her book in a local bookstore.

"Thanks a lot." She could hardly speak, she felt so dismayed.

"You know, you're absolutely right." Angela narrowed her eyes on Georgeanne, who knew she resembled a ripe tomato in spite of her best efforts at ordinariness. "The way that woman writes sounds exactly like the way Georgie talks." She tossed her fuzzy red hair back and intoned, "Hello, Mr. Leno, this is Angela Porter, freelance agent. For a small fee, I can arrange an introduction to that reclusive author everyone is chasing, Ms. Fritzi Field. You can be the first—"

"Cut it out, Angie," Denise said. "You're embarrassing poor Georgie."

"Can't you just see me on the Jay Leno show?" Georgeanne managed. "I'd say about two words and freeze into a neon-red block of ice."

Angela studied Georgeanne. "Actually, you look like the perfect, professional guest."

Georgeanne glanced down at her new yellow jersey dress. She loved yellow, but the color was much too bright to wear for a public appearance. Whenever Georgeanne had to appear on a stage, she took care to dress in something brown. Otherwise, she dominated the stage, thanks to her height.

"My dream is to be interviewed by Oprah Winfrey," Denise said. "Wouldn't I have a fantastic time telling everybody how the world ought to be? Lord, I wish I'd thought of *Faking It* first."

At the moment, Georgeanne wished Denise had, too.

"Oh, not me," Sandra said. "I'd just die if anyone thought I had written that book, much as I agree with what it says. Everyone would assume I was writing about myself."

Georgeanne sucked in her breath. From the way her skin prickled, she knew her complexion turned white, then red.

Angela leaned across the counter and peered at Georgeanne. "Now that I think about it, Georgie has been acting weird ever since Denise started bringing that book to work. She never used to blush this much."

Georgeanne hurried into thoughtless self-defense. "I just don't think sex ought to be discussed in public the way all these shows and books seem to be discussing it these days. It's a private thing between the two people involved."

"That's not what you said last week." Sandra bent her fair head and wrinkled her brow. "Last week, you said it was a good thing that people these days are more open about sex. You said it would prevent lots of bad marriages."

"Well, this week I've changed my mind." Georgeanne knew that if she didn't get control of her complexion and her voice, not to mention her common sense and her memory, her secret would be out. "It must be Denise's habit of reading bits of Fritzi Field to me at odd times. Obviously, it's affecting my brain."

She needed to get herself hypnotized. Anything that might turn off the blushes.

Angela laughed. "It's affected all of us. Why are you so interested in that stupid book, Denise?"

Denise closed the book. She drew her perfect figure to its full height and assumed every bit of the dignity that she could assume when necessary. "If I'd had this book before my husband left me, I'd still be married." She marched out of Georgeanne's office, leaving dismayed silence behind her.

"Oh, wow." Angela stared after Denise. "Denise is one of the sexiest-looking women I've ever seen. Is she telling us she was frigid? That that's why her husband left her?"

"There's no such thing as a frigid woman," Georgeanne said in choked tones. "At least, not many. There are, however, lots of ego-involved men who'd rather blame the woman than their own technique."

"That's exactly what Fritzi Field says," Sandra said.

Georgeanne's breath stopped once more. She needed to muzzle herself. Or else.

"She also says sexual incompatibility is a major cause of trouble between couples." Sandra sounded as shocked as Angela. "She says that the woman is the one who is expected to fix everything, while the man keeps on thinking he's Mr. Super-Stud. That's why Fritzi feels a woman is justified in faking orgasm. She says that if orgasm is all it takes to soothe his ego and make him happy, then why not give it to him?"

Georgeanne debated whether she wanted to sink through the floor or allow herself to feel the satisfaction only an author could feel when a reader agrees with her.

On the whole, she thought sinking through the floor was the better choice. Having her private opinion was one thing, but advising other people was quite another. Georgeanne hadn't discovered until too late that giving public advice carried great mental and emotional responsibility.

She wasn't suited for this. Georgeanne covered her burning face with her hands and wished for oblivion.

"Georgie?" Zane Bryant said. "Are you all right? Is there anything I can do?"

Georgeanne's heart froze. Then it resumed beating at a slightly faster pace. She dropped her hands and turned. "Hello, Doctor. We weren't expecting you this early."

"I cleared my schedule so I could be here the entire weekend." He regarded her with concern over the front counter. "What's wrong?"

"She's had bad news." Angela smiled a greeting at him. "She's just learned she's the number one suspect in the search for the real Fritzi Field."

Georgeanne reacted to the remark the way she would to an unexpected kick to her kneecap. "Don't be ridiculous, Angie. You know very well I'm not the type to write a book."

"You probably could if you wanted to," Sandra said. "Dr. Gant and Dr. Baghri both say you have writing talent. Look at the way donations are pouring in for the Saturday Clinic."

"Fritzi Field?" Zane frowned. "Isn't she the author of that book they're discussing on all the talk shows? The one who advises women on the proper way to fake an orgasm?"

Georgeanne thought about homicide, suicide, bolts of lightning, and meteors from heaven.

"That's the one." Sandra sent Zane a shy smile. "Denise has been bringing the book to work this past week and reading us all the good parts. Poor Georgie is about to die of embarrassment."

Great. Now Zane Bryant would think she was a prude about sex. Georgeanne attempted to calm herself with the thought that if he did, it was probably for the best.

Zane smiled, smoky eyes brightening. Georgeanne stared at his mouth and thought for the second time that afternoon that everything was going black around her.

"I don't blame her," he said. "From what I heard on one of the late shows last night, Fritzi Field is the vanguard of a backlash against the idea that women are just like men and should enjoy casual sex the same way men do."

Georgeanne's mouth dropped open. "What?"

"The idea is that women are fed up with being told how to enjoy sex," Zane said. "They now want to be told how to fake enjoyment so the enjoy-at-all-cost types will leave them alone. At least that's what the psychologist on the show said."

"Oh, heavens," Georgeanne whispered.

"I knew it." Angela bobbed her red head with enthusiasm. "Fritzi Field is the official spokesperson for women who don't like sex. Instead of enjoying it, they'd rather fake it."

"I don't think that's quite what Fritzi Field said." Georgeanne couldn't let this pass unchallenged.

"It wasn't," Sandra chimed in. "Fritzi Field makes it very clear that her book is intended to help women who simply can't have orgasm on demand, and it's affecting their marriages."

The front door opened and a woman entered with two children in tow, one of whom drooped across the woman's shoulder. Immediately behind her followed a man and his little boy.

"Patients," Georgeanne said with profound relief. "Back to work, folks." Angela disappeared into her lab, and Georgeanne smiled at Zane. "Dr. Bryant, make yourself comfortable."

"Actually, I'd prefer to visit with you a little, if I won't be in the way. Dr. Baghri has patients until three, then we're meeting with several county officials."

Georgeanne managed a shaky smile. The sight of Zane Bryant in a dark gray business suit and a red tie did peculiar things to her breathing and her pulse.

"Are you looking forward to painting the clinic this evening, Dr. Bryant?" Sandra bent to check a name off the appointment book and picked up the folders Georgeanne had laid out for her. "My husband and I will be there. Georgie is the best slave driver a group of slaves could have."

"I'm looking forward to it," Zane said.

Georgeanne's color returned to normal. "Wait till you see how much better it looks, Doctor. Mrs. Collins, if you'd like to bring Jennifer and Mary Lou on back, Dr. Gant will be with you in a moment. Mr. Johnson, you may bring Michael on back to Dr. Baghri's office. He needs to talk to you both."

She only needed to get through this weekend, Georgeanne told herself. Once the new clinic site boasted its new coat of paint and opened to the public, Dr. Zane Bryant would return to his practice in Pasadena, and she could return to her usual routine.

Such as it was, now that Fritzi Field's stunning popularity threatened to destroy both her privacy and her sanity.

• • •

Zane noted that Mr. Johnson gazed at Georgeanne the way a dying swan gazed at its mate. Georgeanne didn't notice the man's fixed, longing gaze, and Zane offered a prayer of thanks. He wanted to avoid making a scene this early in the game by officially declaring Georgeanne off-limits to other males.

He waited until Georgeanne sorted the patients into their respective examining rooms before coming around and joining her in her small office. He studied her desk a moment, noting the neat chaos and the way Georgeanne located anything she needed within a second. He also noted the stack of press announcements she addressed.

"Dr. Baghri says you're the one who should be meeting with media representatives," Zane said. "According to him, you tell his story better than he does."

Georgeanne smiled and slipped another envelope into her printer. "Actually, I don't. I just speak with a Southeast Texas accent and all the other Southeast Texans understand me. But there's nothing like hearing Dr. Baghri's story in his own words. It has a special charm, I think."

Zane agreed and studied her bent head. According to Dr. Baghri, Georgeanne had worked as hard as he had to put his idea into operation, but she remained steadfast in refusing to participate in any of the publicity. She had threatened the amused doctor with death and dismemberment if he tried to award her so much as a single rose at the dedication ceremony.

He pulled up the only other chair in Georgeanne's office and sat down opposite her. "I'd like to talk more with you about the nuts and bolts of getting a clinic like Dr. Baghri's off the ground. Will you have dinner with me before we paint the clinic?"

"Of course. We don't start painting until seven."

"In that case, let's leave from here." As Zane had hoped, Georgeanne would never turn down an opportunity to further Dr. Baghri's idea. "I'd like plenty of time to discuss the idea thoroughly."

Georgeanne looked up from her work and rewarded him with a brief, professional smile. "That would be wonderful, Doctor."

"What's all this doctor business?" he asked. "You and I are not on a professional basis, Georgie." That was the first thing he wanted her to understand. "In fact, I hope we're going to become good friends." That formed an approach to the second thing he wanted her to understand.

She smiled without a trace of shyness, much to his pleasure. "Thank you. I hope so, too. But when I'm in the office, it's better to call doctors 'doctor'."

He acceded, so long as she promised to drop it the moment they got outside the office.

"Georgie," Denise called. "About that statement of yours that sex is a private thing between the two people involved. That's completely—oh, hello, Doctor—opposite to what you said last week. Are you sure you don't know more about Fritzi Field than you're letting on?"

Georgeanne promptly turned a color that Zane last remembered seeing when a patient had given him a basket of ripe red strawberries.

"It was a reactionary statement made in self-defense," she said. "If I hear one more word out of anyone in this office about Fritzi Field, I promise you, there will be hell to pay."

"Wouldn't it be wonderful if our Georgie turned out to be Fritzi Field?" Denise said to Zane. "Oprah Winfrey might even call this office."

"Dream on, Denise," Georgeanne said. "How is little Jennifer Collins doing?"

"Little Jenny has another strep throat coming on." Denise leaned over the rear counter of Georgeanne's small office and grinned at Zane. "While Angie was doing the throat swab, Mrs. Collins and I were talking about *Faking It*. Did you know Mrs. Collins—?"

Georgeanne interrupted in what Zane considered an almost frightened way. "Tell Mrs. Collins to try some slippery elm tea for Jenny's throat. Very soothing. By the way, don't forget to bring a scarf for your hair tonight. Paint is going to fly."

Before Denise returned to her post in the examining room, she gave Zane a commiserating wink.

Zane studied Georgeanne. He'd swear she turned away in order to hide her burning cheeks.

Perhaps she needed reassurance that he found her ability to blush charming rather than prudish.

Because Zane felt sure of one thing—Georgeanne Hartfield was no prude, and he intended to prove it very soon.

• • •

Georgeanne's day, in her opinion, had spun out of control.

"It sounds as though Fritzi Field has made a big hit with your friends." Zane helped Georgeanne into his car, an older but well-kept Lincoln Continental, and blocked her hand with his own in order to open the door for her. "They all seem bent upon teasing you about it."

"It's my own fault." Rattled, Georgeanne settled onto the car seat and looked up at him.

He grinned at her as if he knew men usually got out of her way and let her open her own car doors. Georgeanne forbade herself the pleasure of staring at him.

"Denise has been reading choice bits aloud from the book for the past week," she added. "If I didn't blush so easily, they wouldn't have any reason to tease me."

Zane looked down at her with an expression of interest. "What do you think about the book?"

Mercifully, he shut the door and came around to slide in beside her. She watched him and composed a reply in the interval.

"It seems to me that Fritzi Field wrote the book as an analysis of why her own marriage failed, and what she could have done about it," she said. "That's why the book speaks so strongly to certain women and is so annoying to others."

"Do you think so?" Zane sounded fascinated, much to Georgeanne's horror. "That's an interesting theory. I listened to three psychologists arguing for almost an hour last night, and no one ever brought that idea up."

That figured. Georgeanne mentally kicked herself. "I don't know why that occurred to me. I'm probably all wrong."

"You're probably correct." He chuckled. "You'd be a hit on the talk show circuit. You're a better psychologist than the PhD shrinks I saw last night."

Georgeanne suppressed a horrified moan. "You know how it is when a stray thought crosses your mind. Lots of times, that thought is the result of clues your subconscious has been picking up for days. In my case, I've been listening to bits and pieces of that book, along with assorted commentary from my friends, for the past week."

Zane glanced at her, his smoky gray eyes sympathetic. "You have a degree in psychology, according to Dr. Gant. And you've been married, haven't you? Maybe that gives you the background to better understand Fritzi Field's motivations."

Georgeanne turned her face away to hide her burning cheeks. "That may be true, but so have lots of other people. When Fritzi Field finally comes out of the closet, we'll probably be shocked at what she's really like."

Zane drove directly to a nearby family-style Mexican diner and hopped out. Georgeanne realized he expected her to remain seated until he opened the door for her. Her cheeks reddened again at the realization that this man intended to treat her as a date rather than as a colleague.

She felt his gaze upon her while she emerged from his car. The bright yellow jersey dress she wore fell to the middle of her calves, and she wore a pair of highly polished brown boots that matched her hair and complemented the dress. Even though she did not have to worry about exposing too much leg, she still felt almost as if she wasn't wearing enough clothing.

It was ridiculous. Zane Bryant was not here to court her. He was here to learn more about operating a charity clinic.

He took her arm and escorted her inside. His silence allowed her to regain her equanimity.

"I love this restaurant." Georgeanne gazed about happily. "They have a cheese enchilada that's out of this world."

"I'll take your word for it." He placed their order swiftly, asking for the same enchiladas that she had ordered.

Georgeanne looked about at the colorful Mexican decor and felt thoroughly at home. It wasn't often she felt so comfortable with a man. But then, she wasn't with Zane Bryant in the capacity of a date. She'd never have felt this relaxed in the presence of so handsome a man under those circumstances, nor would she have even thought about ordering the cheese enchiladas she loved. She'd have ordered a big salad and starved the rest of the evening so he wouldn't think she ate too much.

"I've ordered a major pizza delivery for ten o'clock," she said. "Don't you think everyone will be hungry about then?"

"Pizza is welcome at any time," Zane said. "Tell me something, Georgie. Will you be available soon to…spend some time with a man who needs your help badly?"

Georgeanne looked across the table at him with a complete lack of self-consciousness. She munched on a tortilla chip she had dipped in salsa and smiled. "Are you thinking about opening a clinic like Dr. Baghri's in Pasadena?"

"Eventually, I hope to do so." He reached for her hand, folding it between both his own. He had to feel her jolt of surprise, even though she didn't withdraw her hand. "You're the most incredible woman I've ever met. How did you get involved in this work?"

Georgeanne looked at her hand, the hand she'd always considered so much bigger than other women's hands. It was positively dwarfed between Zane's two larger hands. "I suppose I got my start with the Humane Society. I have a house at the end of a dead end road in the middle of the rice fields, and people are always dumping unwanted dogs out there. After taking in about six dogs, I realized I had reached my limit."

"I see. So you volunteered to help out at the Society?"

Georgeanne chuckled. "Yes, I volunteered. Somehow, I ended up in a position of authority."

"That's because you work on problems until you find a solution," Zane said.

"Someone has to solve the problems." Georgeanne figured Dr. Baghri had told him that. It was true enough. She had a knack for defining problems and doing what needed to be done about them, probably because she refused to give up.

"Your husband didn't like the time you were spending on volunteer activities?" he asked, in low tones.

Georgeanne looked away, realizing Dr. Baghri had probably told him a few other things. "No, he didn't. He thought..." She swallowed painfully. "He thought he should come first. Which he did, of course, but I could never seem to explain that to him."

"He resented anything that took your time?"

"I'm afraid so." Georgeanne's dark, honest eyes met his. "Some of it was my own fault. I spent a lot of time trying to convince him of the importance of the work I was doing, and it made him unreasonable."

"He was unreasonable to begin with," Zane said in firm tones. "Didn't he have any community projects he was interested in?"

"He didn't believe in community service or volunteering." Georgeanne disliked making the failure of her marriage look as though it was all her ex-husband's fault. "He grew so resentful of my activities, he accused me of using volunteer work to get out of the house and away from him." She added in aching tones, "Toward the end, that became a lot truer than I like to admit."

"Georgie, don't accuse yourself of destroying your marriage. It just isn't true." Zane sounded convinced of that. "You're the kind of person who'd go out of her way just to make someone else feel good, and that includes your ex-husband."

Georgeanne sighed. "I did my best to please him, but I just couldn't stop my work. Not after I had willingly taken on the responsibility." She paused a moment, then went on in low tones. "I don't mean to make you think my volunteer work was the only problem we had. It wasn't. There were," she hesitated, "other ways I didn't please him. I've often thought that if I'd been a better wife in those other ways, the volunteer work wouldn't have mattered."

Zane frowned over this.

Georgeanne realized Dr. Baghri must have told him her ex-husband had left her for another woman, cleaning out their bank account and leaving Georgeanne with nothing but her house in the country. She had done well since her divorce, but Zane probably realized she still blamed herself for the failure of her marriage.

"Georgie, it wasn't your fault. Take it from me, if your husband had been a man, he'd have sat down with you and worked things out." He smiled and shrugged. "My ex-wife was a rising corporate executive. She married me while I was still in medical school because she thought being a doctor's wife would further her career. What she hadn't counted on was the fact that I had no interest in the social aspects of being a doctor. When I went into pediatrics rather than cardiology, it was the end. She filed for divorce as soon as she realized the marriage wasn't performing as planned."

Georgeanne, shocked, murmured something sympathetic. What did the social aspects of physicianhood matter when a woman was married to a man like Zane Bryant?

"I'm afraid I was a big disappointment to her." Zane's voice carried no hint of remorse. "Instead of partying in my spare time, I volunteered at the county charity clinic and spent my weekends doctoring sick children. The truth is, we married for all the wrong reasons, and we soon found out we had little in common."

"I'm sorry," Georgeanne said, meaning it. "Actually, that's what Dr. Gant says about my husband and me. The only thing we had in common was the fact that—that he was taller than I was. Oh, dear, how silly that sounds."

But it was the truth. Much as Georgeanne hated to admit it, Tony Rollins's chief attraction for her had been his size. For once, she'd met a man who made her feel small and fragile.

"Georgie." Zane waited until her attention returned to him, then laced his fingers through hers. "I don't think it's silly at all. I married Roxanne because she made me feel unlike a geeky guy who spent all his time in science labs."

She smiled back at him gratefully, then glanced down in a puzzled way at their locked hands. Zane Bryant might have spent all his time in science labs, but geeky? No way.

"If that's what it takes to get your attention, then I'm glad that I'm taller than you," he said simply.

Chapter 4

Zane noted that Georgeanne blinked at him as if she thought she wasn't hearing correctly, but she smiled naturally. "I'm glad you're tall, too. You can't think how tiresome it is to tower above most men."

She didn't know, he decided. She had no idea how beautiful she was. That had to be why she wasn't picking up on his meaning. Her long curly lashes fluttered as she looked away.

"You can't think how wonderful it is to find a woman who won't make me feel I'm about to crush her or give her a stiff neck," Zane countered. "You're the perfect height, Georgie. Don't ever let anyone tell you otherwise."

Georgeanne looked at him in an uncertain way, then gave him a firm smile. "I won't. The best thing about being tall is that I'm well suited for things like painting and hauling ladders around."

Zane laughed, realizing Georgeanne had long ago accepted the fact that she was constitutionally incapable of sitting back while a man did all the work. If there was work to be done, she probably felt insulted if she wasn't allowed to do her share.

"I'm looking forward to meeting your dogs," he said. "They aren't the kind that chew up any male encroaching on their territory, are they?"

She still didn't take his interest in her personally. Or she refused to. Well, he'd just see about that.

"Basically, they only want to be loved." Georgeanne's face bore a puzzled expression, as if she couldn't imagine why he might want to visit her home. "I only have two dogs now. I've managed to find good homes for the others."

Two cheese enchilada dinners arrived, and Georgeanne looked thankful to have something other than his face to concentrate on. Before he could drag her attention back to him, someone interrupted.

"Excuse me." A teenage girl stood beside their table, gazing reverently at Zane. "May I please have your autograph?"

Zane glanced up and smiled. "I'm not Hunter Howell, you know."

The girl gave a deep sigh and held out her book anyway. "You're not?"

"I'm not." Zane signed his name in a thick, dark scrawl across a blank sheet of notebook paper. "I'm just a doctor. Not a very exciting person at all."

The girl accepted the notebook, studied the signature, and went back to her parents' table with a posture eloquent of disappointment.

"You have the signature of a true doctor," Georgeanne said, with her deep rich chuckle. "I suppose that's why she believed you."

Zane laughed. "You should know. You've been seeing it long enough. You're part of the reason why I decided to come see Dr. Baghri's clinic for myself. I wanted to get a look at the woman who wrote me so faithfully."

"In that case, I hope you weren't disappointed." She looked, as he had thought she might, totally astonished. "I'd hate to think my personal appearance put you off participating in Dr. Baghri's clinic."

"Oh, I wasn't disappointed, Georgie. I wasn't disappointed at all." He smiled at her, a slow, hot smile that came straight from thoughts of how she would look without her clothes. "You were exactly what I hoped for, right down to the tips of those boots."

Georgeanne appeared to stop breathing while she stared at him.

Zane looked back at her. Obviously, he had taken her by surprise, and whatever she expected from him, she had not expected an interest in her. He noted, with amusement, that she appeared to be searching her brain for an alternate meaning to his words.

"I'm glad," she said at length. "Does it bother you to have so many people mistake you for your brother?"

Zane liked her quiet acceptance of his statement. Now was not the time to push her further, not when they were due at the new clinic site within an hour. "As a matter of fact, I had no idea Hunter Howell existed until I had people on the street ask me for my autograph after *Sunfire Down* made him a star. That's what led me to discover I had a brother."

Georgeanne nodded sympathetically. "It must have been a real shock to see yourself on a movie screen."

"It was." Zane hadn't told anyone the entire story of discovering his brother, but found himself telling Georgeanne everything he'd done and felt. "Having a twin is the sort of thing every kid dreams about, but I never really expected to find one when I checked the adoption records."

"You must have been very angry." Georgeanne lowered her gaze to her plate. "It seems so unfair to separate identical twin brothers."

"I was pretty angry at first," Zane admitted. "Then I realized how lucky I'd been. Hunter was adopted by a couple who fell upon hard times. He'd been badly abused, while I had received every advantage, including a lot of love."

Georgeanne's dark-brown eyes actually filled with tears. "What sort of man did he become?"

Zane wanted to touch her face and kiss away the tears. "He's surprisingly normal, considering." He longed to cradle her head on his shoulder and tell her all the things he wasn't saying—all the emotions she seemed to be picking up from the ether. "You'll have to judge for yourself. Believe it or not, we've become close friends."

"Why shouldn't you? It's my understanding that identical twins usually wind up in similar circumstances in spite of totally different upbringings." She smiled suddenly. "In fact, I'd be willing to bet a reasonable sum on the assumption that he's into hands-on volunteer work himself."

Zane's gray eyes widened. "How did you know?" He should have realized Georgeanne Hartfield had a sixth sense when it came to people and emotions. "Don't say anything, will you? Hunt would kill me if he thought I'd let out his dirty little secret."

"That's right. Hunter Howell makes his living being a tough guy without a conscience, doesn't he?" Georgeanne laughed, a delicious ripple of sound that traveled through Zane like the vibrations of a stringed instrument. "I'll have to go see his latest movie and judge for myself what he's really like."

"Fine. I'll pick you up tomorrow night at seven. The show starts at seven-thirty."

Georgeanne's mouth dropped open, but she shut it again quickly. "Doctor, you're forgetting yourself. You're a member of my painting crew, and my painting crew does not see movies when there is painting to be done. I have been known to conduct hangings and public whippings over such infractions."

"My deepest, most heartfelt apologies." He grinned at her, fully aware that she had been shocked at the invitation. "It's just that I'd really like to know your impression of Hunter." He added, "Seeing that you're such a good judge of people..."

"I'm no better a judge than you, Doc—Zane." She changed the subject, and he allowed it, for now. "Dr. Baghri says you're involved in quite a few volunteer efforts yourself."

"When a man feels profoundly lucky in life, it's natural to want to give something back," Zane said.

He questioned her about her training as a psychologist and her current choice of work then listened intently to what she had to say about her interest in children, the family home she'd inherited in the middle of the rice fields, and her instant need for a job after her divorce.

As he had hoped, she described a happy childhood—up until the day both her parents had died in a car wreck and she went to live with her father's brother. She glossed over that by asking Zane about his career in medicine.

Zane was conscious for once that the woman he was telling his life story to was really interested. He had never told anyone about the incident that led him into pediatrics, but he found himself telling Georgeanne.

"It was a case like the ones that inspired Dr. Baghri to open his Saturday Children's Clinic." He wondered if he could drown in Georgeanne's velvety eyes. "A couple brought an unconscious little boy, who was in a deep diabetic coma, into the Emergency Room one night. When I finally got him stabilized and went out to lecture his parents about why they had waited so long to see a doctor, I discovered they were hard-working people with no insurance who couldn't afford regular doctor visits. I learned a lot that night about pride and compassion."

"Those are the people Dr. Baghri wants to help." Georgeanne's voice quivered with emotion. "They can afford the twenty dollars at the Saturday Clinic, and their pride isn't attacked."

Zane nodded. He wondered if Georgeanne knew how beautiful she was when emotion animated her face. "The people who need help these days are those caught in the middle."

"Are you still treating the boy?" Georgeanne asked.

"Of course." Zane laughed at her expectant attitude. "I charge twenty dollars a visit, which covers a supply of insulin and syringes and his checkup."

Georgeanne lowered her gaze to her plate, smiling.

"That's why I'll never be a particularly rich doctor. But you don't care about that, do you?" He stared at Georgeanne and wondered how she was going to react when he kissed her. Because he was going to, very soon now, and he was already looking forward to it tremendously.

Georgeanne laughed. "I'll never be a particularly rich secretary-receptionist, and for much the same reason."

"According to Dr. Gant, you could have taken a much higher paying job last year with an advertising agency in Beaumont." Zane wondered why Georgeanne's expressive face whitened suddenly. "Why didn't you?"

"I didn't want that long drive every day," she said. "Also, I prefer lower-stress work."

"I see." He thought he did. Georgeanne was the kind of woman who valued working with friends and with the patients she'd gotten to know. "You don't consider the extra work you're doing for Dr. Baghri's clinic stress?"

"Dr. Baghri's clinic is a lot of fun." Georgeanne contemplated the dessert menu a moment. "My idea of stress is a flu or measles epidemic. Besides, if I'd taken the advertising job, I wouldn't have been in on Dr. Baghri's Saturday Clinic. I've never enjoyed anything so much."

"And I'd never have met you." Zane willed her to believe him. "Do you believe in destiny, Georgie?"

She looked at him, then away. "I'm not sure. There are so many meanings that can be attached to that word."

He leaned forward, shoving his plate aside. "Do you believe there's a man out there for you? One created especially for you?"

"Heavens, Zane." Georgeanne's lashes fluttered uncertainly. "What a question." She thought a moment. "At one time, I did believe that, but now, I'm not sure. I think the proverb: 'Love isn't so much about finding the right person as it is being the right person' is more likely to result in true happiness."

Right there, under his watchful eyes, Georgeanne swallowed and looked away. Zane wondered what on earth had crossed her mind to make her react that way.

"In short, you've been disillusioned." Zane smiled. "Georgie, I'm going to do my best to make you believe in destiny. In another week, you can report on any changes in your beliefs."

• • •

Georgeanne drove herself home and wondered what on earth Zane meant. His words sounded like a vow, but she certainly wasn't the kind of woman who inspired men to go around vowing to change a woman's perceptions of the world.

When she arrived at the clinic site prepared to paint, and found Zane and Dr. Baghri already present, she soon realized her perceptions of the world were indeed changing, and that Zane Bryant was behind the change. He would be lucky if she didn't strangle him before the night was out.

"You're not getting on that ladder, Georgie," Zane said in stern tones. "Don't even think about it."

Georgeanne, comfortable in a man's work shirt and her old painting jeans, turned to stare at him. Zane had driven her back to the Gant Clinic to pick up her car then had gone to Dr. Baghri's house, where he was staying the weekend. He had changed into jeans and an old knit shirt that outlined his powerful shoulders and enhanced his commanding presence.

Georgeanne did not consider herself a particularly commandable woman. Moreover, in this case she was the commander, and Zane was one of her commandees.

"Zane, I am painting this ceiling." She indicated the ceiling in the clinic's waiting room. "Tall as I am, I still cannot paint it if I stand on the floor. Besides, you were assigned to paint the examining room. Why are you in here bugging me?"

"I'm in here because I'm going to paint the ceiling while you paint the windows."

"I do not do windows," Georgeanne said with dignity. "I do ceilings." She gestured at her hair. It was pulled back in a heavy ponytail for the occasion, and she had tied a scarf over as much of her hair as she could cover.

"You don't do ceilings tonight. Not after you spent half of last night scrubbing these floors. You're exhausted, whether you know it or not. Come away from that ladder."

Georgeanne felt her eyes open wide. "Exhausted? Me?"

Zane's face reflected his struggle not to laugh, she saw with resentment.

He climbed the ladder himself. "Yes, you. In case you're thinking I've gotten above myself, let me tell you that Dr. Baghri and Dr. Gant both agree with me."

Georgeanne took a moment to master herself. One did not argue with doctors in public. It ruined the godlike image so dear to the medical heart. "What you mean is that you bullied them into agreeing with you. Very well, Doctor. If you want to hog the ceiling, you may do so. I'll take the examining room."

"Angela has already agreed to do the examining room." Zane directed a charming smile down at her from atop the ladder Georgeanne should have been on. "I wanted a chance to talk to you while we work."

Georgeanne regarded him with considerable suspicion.

Zane broke into unabashed laughter. "Not many people argue with you, do they?"

"They know better." Georgeanne smiled reluctantly.

"Paint the windows, Georgie," Sandra struck in. "Dr. Bryant is right. If you aren't exhausted, you should be."

"The day scrubbing a mere floor exhausts me is the day I pick out my coffin." Georgeanne picked up a sash brush and a can of paint with ill grace. "I can see the composition of my painting crew needs some reassessment."

"Forget the windows, Georgie," Zane said. "Why don't you fetch your whip and walk around keeping everyone's nose to the grindstone. We don't want you to collapse before the clinic's grand opening."

Outraged, Georgeanne stared up at him. "I have never collapsed in my life. I do not intend to start now. As for exhausted—"

"Oh, shut up and do what he says, Georgie," Angela called from the doorway into one of the examining rooms. "You are tired, whether you admit it or not. I saw you yawning into your sleeve several times this morning."

"That was because—" Georgeanne broke off.

"If you're intending to claim you were yawning because I was reading choice excerpts aloud from Fritzi Field's book, I'm calling you a liar to your face." Denise Devereaux appeared in the doorway, dressed in disreputable old clothes and grinning. "You were as interested as the rest of us, you prevaricator, you."

Georgeanne knew her heart had just jolted to a dead halt. "If you intend to enliven my paint-in by reading aloud pieces out of that book…"

"Who, me? Would I do that in mixed company?" Denise laughed. "Besides, I wouldn't risk getting paint on my precious book. Where do you want me, Georgie?"

"Dr. Gant could use some help in the second examining room," Zane said, indicating it. "His wife had a meeting tonight."

Georgeanne opened her mouth, then shut it again when Zane spoke up. She shrugged with good-natured acceptance. At least Denise hadn't brought *Faking It* along.

"Uh-oh." Denise winked at Georgeanne. "Looks like we've got a new slave driver."

"I'm getting into practice," Zane said. "Go sit down somewhere, Georgie. You do look tired."

"I do not look tired."

Georgeanne gave up. What good was claiming she felt as energetic as ever when no one believed her? Somehow, Zane had convinced everyone that she was in danger of imminent collapse. Everyone was very solicitous of her health.

Talk about a revolting development, Georgeanne thought. She always worked steadily until she got things done, and she never over-tired herself.

Zane painted the ceiling for the next two hours, while she puttered around trying to find a job worthy of her efforts. Never before had she experienced a situation like this one, where the work had literally been pulled out from under her.

"Settle down, Georgie." Zane looked down at her, grinning as if he knew exactly what she was thinking. "You can kill me later."

"I don't think I can wait until later. I think I'd better kill you now, while you're in a precarious position." She pretended to shake the ladder he was standing on. "This has got to be one of the most boring evenings of my existence. What did you tell them before I got here?"

Zane looked down at her a moment, then laid his paintbrush carefully across the top of his open paint can. "Let's walk outside a moment and I'll tell you. These paint fumes are finally getting to me."

Georgeanne had unboarded and scrubbed all the windows, and they all stood open. The clinic's electricity had been restored, and electric fans buzzed in each window. Still, the heavy, fresh scent of latex paint was overpowering. She nodded and moved slowly toward the door. A few minutes of outside air would be welcome.

She had discarded her scarf since there wasn't any need to wear a scarf if she wasn't allowed to do any painting. Her ponytail brushed her shoulder blades as she stepped outside into the cool, night air. Seconds later, she felt Zane's big hand in the center of her back, guiding her toward the group of tallow trees near the road.

"I'm really not tired, Zane," she said in mild tones. "If it comes to that, there's nothing more tiring than standing around doing nothing while everyone else works."

"If you're not exhausted, you should be," he said grimly. "When I found out you'd spent five hours scrubbing that floor last night, I was ready to send you home to bed. Be thankful I didn't do just that."

They had reached the narrow asphalt road. Georgeanne gazed around and breathed in the rich, earthy scent of spring, noting with delight the early fireflies that dotted the lower level of the surrounding fields and tallow trees. The peaceful sight and deep breathing calmed her nerves, not to mention helped stifle the impulse to tell Zane exactly what she thought of his managing ways.

"Zane, I am not some delicate little creature—"

"Thank God for that," Zane interrupted. "Just don't expect me to stand by while you do your best to exhaust yourself."

The next thing Georgeanne knew, his arms went around her and he pulled her solidly against him. She gasped with shock, and his mouth descended on hers.

Georgeanne knew she must be dreaming. This could not possibly be happening. She stood in the middle of the rice fields, being thoroughly kissed by a man who looked like a movie star, and the only thing she could do about it was kiss him back.

She had been kissed before, kissed with passion, kissed with need, even kissed with joy, but she had never been kissed like this. What the difference was, Georgeanne couldn't have said, but there was a difference. The trouble was, she was so surprised she couldn't think.

Zane's hands traveled up her back. He pressed her against him, so that her curves fit perfectly into the hard hollows of his body and kissed her again. One of his big hands pulled the rubber band out of her hair, freeing the thick brown mass to his touch. He worked his fingers into her hair and tilted her head to meet him. This time he parted her lips in a way that told Georgeanne he knew what he was doing. Nothing mattered except the feelings that exploded across every nerve ending she had.

Georgeanne's head fell back in acquiescence. Any thought she had of protesting the kiss evaporated before it had fully formed. Her arms rose to wrap themselves around his neck without any conscious direction from her. The next thing she knew, she kissed him back with enthusiasm.

• • •

Zane knew immediately when Georgeanne got over her surprise. Her body softened, and her lips parted to accept his tongue with an honesty and passion that enchanted him. His hand stayed buried as deeply in her hair as he wanted to bury himself in her. He slid his hand down the curve of her hip. She felt so good in his arms—just right, in fact. No woman had ever fit into his arms the way Georgeanne did. She had to realize that.

He lifted his head and waited until her lashes fluttered up and Georgeanne's dark eyes gazed into his. Even in the darkness, he could see that her face reflected dazed passion and mute acceptance "Georgie, I want you," he said.

Georgeanne's expression altered, but she said nothing. Perhaps she didn't know what to say.

She had to feel his desire. She probably felt everything, close as he held her against him. He knew of no reason why she might withhold herself from him, but if there was a reason, he wanted to hear it now.

"I can't see pretending," he went on. "You've got to know it sooner or later. Frankly, I'd rather it be sooner."

"I—Zane, I—" Georgeanne broke off. To his surprise, she sounded unlike her usual decisive self.

"I realize you don't know me very well. That's why I'm not going to push you. At least, not much," he added with wry humor. "But I am going to be with you a lot. As much as you'll let me, in fact. Will you let me take you to see Hunter's movie?"

"I—yes. I'd like that very much."

"Good." He laughed suddenly, an exultant, boyish laugh. For a moment, he had feared she intended to turn him down. "I can't wait until Hunter meets you. He's going to love you. No, scratch that. He's sure to recognize the fact that you're off limits to him. Hunt's an honorable sort in spite of that bad boy image."

"Oh." Georgeanne sounded like a woman who had no idea why she had said yes, he noted. Perhaps she thought things were happening too fast between them. "I'm glad to know that."

Some interesting item must have passed through her brain, because she went from biting her lip to a sudden sigh of acceptance. She almost smiled, and he wondered how soon he could coax her into telling him her thoughts.

"Georgie, you're priceless." He laughed again and tightened his hold on her. "We're going to be good together. You'll see."

Georgeanne stirred in his arms. "What makes you so sure?" she asked, with wry humor. "What happens when you discover the truth—that I'm a managing sort of woman who doesn't take orders well?"

"I can live with being managed," he said, with suitable gravity. "So long as you can live with taking occasional orders from me when I decide you're being taken advantage of."

Georgeanne looked at him with an expression he interpreted as disbelief. "Can you live with the fact that I may ignore the orders upon occasion?"

"Wait a minute." Zane laughed. "I'll have to think on that one." He held her and pretended to think deeply. The feel of

Georgeanne's generous curves and soft warmth against his body set fire to his blood, and this was only the first time he'd kissed her. "As a doctor, I'm not accustomed to having my orders ignored. I can't be answerable for my actions if such an unheard-of thing should happen."

"Uh-oh." Georgeanne bent her head a little, and a small smile curved her lovely mouth. "We might have an impasse here. If you did something outrageous, I'd have to retaliate."

"If the retaliation involves kissing me into submission, I can live with it." Zane grinned. "So long as you think you can live with the fact that I would have to respond to your retaliation."

Georgeanne looked up and smiled back. "In that case, we have a deal. I get to ignore your orders, and I get to kiss you into submission in retaliation for your reaction to my flouting of your orders."

"What?" He wondered what on earth that meant. "Never mind. So long as it involves getting kissed into submission by you, I'll sign anything." Zane lowered his mouth to hers again. Georgeanne had the most kissable mouth he'd ever seen, and he intended to take advantage of that fact at every chance he got.

Headlights appeared far down the road and came steadily closer. Zane reluctantly loosened his hold on Georgeanne while she peered at her watch, holding it toward the headlights.

"It's time for the pizza delivery." Georgeanne sounded disappointed, which delighted him. "We'd better go back inside."

For a moment he debated kissing her again, but the pizza driver was almost upon them, so they walked back to the clinic. He managed to keep her hand in his. He wanted everyone inside the clinic to know Georgeanne belonged to him, whether she knew it yet or not.

Zane let go her hand and draped his arm across her shoulders as she stepped in the door. She headed back toward the old laboratory, and he remained beside her, so close his body brushed against hers.

"There you are, Georgie," Denise said.

Zane saw that Dr. Gant, Dr. Baghri, Denise, Angela, and Sandra's husband, Bobby Whitney, stood in a semicircle, paintbrushes in hand, obviously in the midst of an important discussion.

"Georgie." Denise sounded insistent. "Didn't Fritzi Field say it's almost impossible for a man to tell whether or not a woman is faking an orgasm? She's a psychologist, and she should know, right?"

To Zane's intense interest, Georgeanne turned the color of a boiled lobster. Her face spoke eloquently of a desire to vanish into the woodwork.

She said in choked tones, "Really?"

"You're a psychologist, too," Denise reminded her. "You know as much as Fritzi Field does. What do you say, Georgie?"

Chapter 5

Georgeanne felt Zane's hand tighten on her shoulder. Where were lightning bolts and quicksand floors when you needed them?

"Why are you asking Georgie when there is a roomful of doctors standing here just dying to give you a technical opinion on the matter?" Zane asked.

Denise looked scornful. "Anyone who works for doctors knows they don't know anything about sex. I want somebody's opinion who's qualified. Georgie, what do you say?"

There was a moment of stunned silence, then everyone burst into laughter.

Georgeanne laughed with them in spite of her strong urge to bolt from the room. "I may be qualified as a psychologist, but I think that particular question ought to be answered by someone with a lot of training in anatomy and physiology."

"You're just trying to get out of answering," Denise accused. "You've been taking evasive action ever since I started talking about Fritzi Field's book. Well, you aren't getting out of it this time. Speak, oracle. Tell us the truth about men's much-vaunted perspicacity when it comes to reading women."

All too conscious of the many pairs of male eyes upon her, Georgeanne produced a great, universal truth. "I think it depends on the particular man involved."

Denise, joined by Angela, groaned in loud disgust.

"Talk about a cop-out," Angela said, snickering.

"I don't want another one of your evasions," Denise said. "I want an answer. What do you say about most men? Do they, or don't they, know when a woman is faking it?"

Georgeanne wished in vain for an earthquake. Or better yet, a meteor. Anything spectacular that would make everyone forget about Fritzi Field's sexual advice to women and Georgeanne Hartfield's psychology degree.

When nothing spectacular happened to save her, Georgeanne cleared her throat. "I...Well, since I haven't personally—er—tested a viable sample of men, I can't speak with any authority."

"No one's asking you to," Denise pointed out. "All I want is a psychologist's learned opinion on the subject. Now speak up, Georgie. Do they or don't they know?"

"They don't," Georgeanne said and wished she'd answered the opposite. She broke free of Zane's grasp and snatched up her purse. "Excuse me, please. The pizza delivery is here."

"That's a lot of bull." Bobby Whitney looked through the doors toward the waiting room, where his wife, Sandra, painted a wall. "I'd sure know if my wife faked it. There's no way I could help knowing."

"Now you just hold it right there, Georgie Hartfield." Denise grabbed for her. "You've got to explain that answer."

"Not me." Georgeanne made a break for the door. "The mark of a truly learned psychologist is that she knows when to flee the scene."

"Making love is an obsessive American topic," Dr. Baghri observed. "Everyone has an opinion. Everyone wants to go on television and talk about his opinion. When do they have time to actually make love?"

Georgeanne heard this with relief as she fled toward the waiting room and the front entrance. Dr. Baghri was sure to favor the group with an Indian male's position on America's idea of sex as public recreation. If that didn't put everyone back to work, nothing would.

"Here, Georgie, let me get that," Zane said from just behind her. "Since I've usurped your position as official slave driver, I may as well pay for the slaves' food as well." He produced his wallet before she could fumble through her purse and received the four large pizza boxes and the cardboard caddy of soft drinks. "Are you, by any chance, running out on the discussion back there?" He indicated the laboratory, where loud voices issued forth in passionate disagreement.

"Of course I am. Aren't you?" Georgeanne managed a weak smile. "Denise has been reading pieces of that book to us all week. If I hear one more word about it, I'll go nuts."

She'd go more than nuts. She'd go ballistic. She'd suffer a core meltdown. She might just flat die.

"It sounds like an interesting book." Zane handed the cardboard holder of soft drinks to her, his smoky eyes warm with amusement. "I'll have to buy a copy. From what I heard on TV last night, it's got every talk show and every psychologist and sex therapist in the country up in arms."

"That's what I tried to tell Denise." Georgeanne knew she must resemble the bottom end of a thermometer. "Authors make their money by writing controversial books that give talk show hosts something titillating to talk about. Fritzi Field probably researched the market for two years before she conceived a sufficiently controversial idea and sat down to write the actual book."

"I don't think so," Sandra chimed in.

Georgeanne started. She had forgotten Sandra's presence.

Sandra shoved back the paint-splattered blue cap on her soft blonde hair. "I read the foreword of Denise's copy this afternoon, and my impression is that Fritzi Field is a woman who has suffered personally. It's the only way she can write the way she does."

"That's how authors always write." Georgeanne knew she ought to shut up, but somehow she found it impossible. "If they can't connect with their audience on a very personal level, they don't sell many books. It's that simple."

Sandra laid her brush aside and came toward them to lift a couple of pizza boxes off the stack in Zane's arms. "Well, you would probably know more than I would about that. You're an author yourself, aren't you? Dr. Gant said you've sold lots of magazine articles."

Georgeanne wished yet again for a laser-targeted meteor, one that would zip right through the roof and land on her head. She had to stop talking. The more she spoke, no matter how innocuous her statements, the damning evidence added up. Already, Zane gazed at her in a fascinated way now that he had learned the one thing she'd rather have kept a secret from him—that she was a writer who knew the rudiments of selling her writing. If he should put two and two together, the expression on his face when he looked at her would alter radically.

"Magazine articles are vastly different from books," Georgeanne stated and hoped she sounded like an authority. "That particular book probably had an agent hyping it to all the publishers, and it probably garnered a huge advance when it sold. The author is very likely well-known within the publishing industry, even though she—or he—is remaining anonymous to the public at large."

"But the principle is still the same." Zane smiled warmly at her. "The best writers have a very personal style. From what I'm told, Fritzi Field has a style somewhere between a mother and Dr. Marcus Welby."

Georgeanne paled and hurried to speak, but it was too late.

"That's what we all agreed this afternoon." Denise appeared beside Zane. She sniffed the air enthusiastically and lifted a pizza box from Sandra's hands. "Fritzi writes exactly the way Georgie speaks. One minute, she sounds like your doctor and the next minute, she's your mother. You feel like you're being personally instructed."

"Is that right?" Zane's interested gaze rested on Georgeanne's burning cheeks. "In that case, I'll definitely have to buy a copy of that book. I'll read anything that sounds as if Georgie could have written it."

These words would have sent Georgeanne's heart into a pleasant flutter if they'd referred to anything she had written other than *Faking It*. "I hardly think—"

"You'd better buy a copy then," Denise said, "because *Faking It* sounds exactly like something Georgie could write."

Georgeanne considered quitting her job and moving someplace where she had no friends to embarrass her. Say, the North Pole. Or better yet, the South Pole. It was further away. "Thanks a lot, Denise. If I get a call next week from Oprah Winfrey, I'm handing it over to you."

"I wish you would." Denise sat down on the newspaper-covered floor and popped the lid off a cup of soft drink. "I'll say I'm Fritzi's manager, and that I simply must meet Oprah personally before I can allow Fritzi to come on the show."

The cheesy smell of pizza permeated the clinic, overriding the odor of paint and enticing the workers into the waiting room. Soon, people sat all over the floor eating pizza, sipping soft drinks, and arguing about Fritzi Field.

"You can mark my words," Bobby Whitney said. "She's a feminist-man-hater with hairy legs. She's probably ugly on top of that."

"You should read the foreword of her book," Sandra smiled fondly at Bobby. "I think she must have suffered a lot in her own marriage. She sounded like she was speaking from experience."

"That's exactly what I think," Denise proclaimed. As the only person present who had actually read the book, Denise's opinion carried weight. "The whole time I was reading, I was just crying for her. You could tell her poor little heart had been broken, and that she was lamenting that she hadn't known then what she knows now."

Georgeanne stared at the floor. Lord, why hadn't she realized how exposed she'd feel with that book in print?

Because she had never really expected anyone to publish her book, much less read it—that was why. Writing it had been wonderful therapy, but the problem with being a writer was that said writer didn't know when to let well enough alone.

She'd just had to query an agent after doing all that work. When the agent showed interest, she'd been stupid enough to submit the manuscript. When she received an offer, she'd been so surprised, she automatically said yes to everything.

The whole thing just went to prove what she had suspected for some time. The only fate around was a thing of evil that had it in for Georgeanne Hartfield.

Georgeanne looked up and discovered Zane's interested gaze resting on her cheeks. She was probably changing colors like a strobe light. She just hoped she could think of some believable reason for it. Something told her he wouldn't buy the idea that talking about sex embarrassed her.

"Georgie, I want you to read it next," Denise said. "When you get through, I want to know what you think about what Fritzi has to say. You're the only one of us who has the same training Fritzi has."

Georgeanne lost what was left of her appetite. The more likenesses of her opinions to those of Fritzi Field her friends spotted, the more tenuous her position. What if Zane should realize who Fritzi Field really was?

Georgeanne sucked in her breath. Surely she wasn't expecting a man like Zane Bryant to remain interested in her for long just because he'd kissed her and said he wanted her.

She let her breath out slowly. In spite of her training in psychology and her personal experience, she was just like any other woman. She wanted happily-ever-after every time a good-looking man made a mild pass at her.

"I'll be glad to," she said, with credible calm. "As soon as things settle down with the clinic—"

"Oh, no, you don't. You're going to read this book, or I'll come sit on you personally." Denise sounded determined on that much. "I'm going to hear some intelligent discussion of the ideas in here if I have to go on a talk show myself."

To Georgeanne's relief, attention shifted from her to Denise as a possible guest for an Oprah Winfrey interview. She nibbled a slice of pizza with a total lack of appetite.

"In that case, I'll be a gentleman and buy a copy of the book myself," Zane said. "If Georgie's going to read it, I'll read it along with her. What do you say, Georgie?"

He had linked the two of them together into a couple. Georgeanne's cheeks reddened yet again. "You're going to have about as much free time as I will these next few weeks. Are you sure you want to buy a book you won't have time to read?"

Zane chuckled and reached for another slice of pizza. "Far be it from me to deprive an author of her royalties."

"Good for you," Denise said. "Believe me, Fritzi Field deserves support. You can mark my words, lots of women are going to owe their marriages to her."

Naturally, this statement provoked another argument over whether or not a man could detect a woman's deceit in intimacy. Georgeanne maintained silence. Not for anything was she going to get involved in that again.

To her increasing discomfort, Zane listened to the argument eddying around them and watched her face. No doubt he had never seen a woman before whose complexion registered her thoughts so clearly. He had to realize Fritzi Field's book embarrassed the living daylights out of her for some reason. Now he intended to read the book and find out why.

Georgeanne wondered, with a sinking heart, what he would think if he ever found out the truth. If, that is, he stuck around long enough to find out the truth.

• • •

Georgeanne spent the next day in a haze of happiness. Zane lost no opportunity to let everyone know she was his, and to her surprise, everyone connected with the clinic accepted the situation without surprise. In fact, her friends seemed to think Zane just might be worthy of her. It provided Georgeanne with a whole new outlook on herself as a desirable woman.

Zane hadn't cared who had been watching when he walked her outside to her vehicle the night before. Around them, the other volunteers were climbing into their cars and preparing to leave, but Georgeanne might as well have been alone with Zane for all the notice either took of their surroundings.

"You're tired, whether you know it or not," Zane had said. "I'll call you to make sure you get home okay, then I want you going straight to bed. Doctor's orders."

"Far be it from me to ignore a doctor's orders," Georgeanne had replied lightly.

Her heart beat rapidly in a manner totally unlike itself. Georgeanne wondered what was wrong with her. Perhaps she was developing an arrhythmia.

Zane laid one large hand on her shoulder and let his fingertips caress her neck. "That's what I like to see, a patient who knows when the doctor has her best interests at heart." He brought his hand around, cupping her neck lightly while his index fingertip stroked her full mouth and outlined her lips. "But you're looking at a doctor with a problem," he added.

Georgeanne's breath was almost gone. Who could breathe while having the tender edge of her lips teased by an expert finger?

"What," she halted a moment to savor the sensation, "seems to be the problem, Doctor?"

"I need a kiss."

What remained of Georgeanne's breath left in a hiss. "You do?"

"I do. Do you think you could oblige?" He smiled the smile of a dark angel who offered temptation in a most enticing package.

Georgeanne stared into his eyes, mesmerized. "I could try."

"I have a feeling you're the cure to any problem I've got." Zane slipped his arms around her waist. "Georgie, you're so beautiful."

Georgeanne started to deny any claim to beauty, but Zane's mouth covered hers before she could speak. She forgot her beauty, or lack thereof, in testing the warm silky texture of his hair and the hard feel of the muscles in his neck.

Zane's tongue stroked hers, encouraging her to explore his mouth the way he explored hers, and his big hands molded her against his body. She felt his desire for her and trembled. The amazing thing was, she liked knowing he wanted her, and she wanted to satisfy that desire.

Georgeanne broke away from the spell cast by his mouth, blinking with dismay. She'd never wanted to satisfy a man's desire before. She had feared that desire, because she knew she lacked what it took to satisfy it.

"What's wrong, Georgie?" Zane touched her face gently. "Am I scaring you?"

Georgeanne looked away. "Nothing is wrong, Zane. It's just that I—that I—I guess it's been a long time since I've been kissed. I don't quite know how to behave."

"You're doing beautifully, Georgie. You're perfect." Zane proved it with another gentle kiss. "This is between us. You and me. No ghosts, and no regrets. Okay?"

She swallowed, breathing hard. "Okay."

His words registered at last. Zane thought her hesitation lay in memories of her marriage. In a way it did, but not the way he thought. She would have groaned aloud if his mouth hadn't covered hers in another tender kiss.

"Now get home and get to bed, or the doctor will have to write you out a stronger prescription."

Georgeanne had done as he instructed, largely because she was too bemused to do anything else. Zane was used to giving orders and having them obeyed. The problem was, Georgeanne liked obeying orders from him a lot more than she should, especially when she knew she would see him again on Sunday.

• • •

Georgeanne glanced around, well pleased, at the Sunday afternoon activities. While the other volunteers finished painting the inside of the clinic, Zane had brought a stack of ropes and saws and worked steadily at removing the crop of fast-growing tallow trees that had sprung up around the building and encroached on the edges of the small shell-covered parking lot.

Georgeanne joined him outside, where she scraped and painted the woodwork around the windows. The beautiful late spring weather held, and the sun shone brightly, bringing out the bright green of the tree leaves surrounding them.

Georgeanne enjoyed watching Zane silhouetted against the sky as he stood on the clinic's flat roof and worked an electric power saw. He removed limb after limb from the trees that grew beside the roof, then began work on one big limb that stretched across the roof.

Georgeanne tried not to stare at him. He wore a blue T-shirt that accentuated the powerful muscles of his shoulders and arms and made his smoky eyes look blue. The rippling motion of those muscles as he worked the saw and the ropes fascinated Georgeanne. She forced herself to concentrate on her paintbrush.

"Would you mind calling one of the men out to help me with this, Georgie," Zane called.

Georgeanne glanced up. He had hooked a complicated series of ropes to the limb and was prepared to saw it through. "What do you need?"

"I need a man to pull this rope to swing the limb away from the roof when it starts to fall. Not you, Georgie."

"Be reasonable, Zane. I'm taller than both the men present, and probably stronger. Throw me that rope."

Zane scowled down at her. "I will not. Call Dr. Baghri or Dr. Gant."

"Now, Zane, if you weren't present, I'd be sawing those trees down myself. Throw me that rope." She laughed up at him, enjoying the way he tried to take care of her, even though anyone could see she didn't need it.

"Georgie, you're about to witness some of my unreasonable behavior brought about by your failure to follow my orders."

"What is it with doctors? They seem to have a problem with thinking they can snap orders at people when they aren't in a medical setting."

"This is a clinic, isn't it?"

"It won't be a clinic until the dedication ceremony one week from today." Georgeanne gazed up and marveled again at the picture he presented.

"This was a medical clinic, and it is about to be a medical clinic again. This is a medical setting, and I am a medical doctor. I have the degrees and the years of penal servitude to prove it. Therefore, when I speak, underlings such as yourself should hop to obey."

"Sez who?" Georgeanne put her hands on her hips and came to stand directly beneath him, grinning.

Zane seized a pair of ropes that were slung over tree limbs in his large hands and grinned back at her. "Sez me. Punishment for this insubordination awaits. Look out below."

To Georgeanne's astonishment, he used the ropes to rappel down from the roof as he spoke. The next instant, he was beside her on the ground. He let go the ropes and grabbed for her.

Georgeanne did the only thing that occurred to her. She broke and ran, laughing with newfound joy and excitement.

Zane followed on her heels. Georgeanne soon realized that he was letting her escape capture long enough to reach a secluded spot among a grove of tallow trees lining one of the rice fields. The moment she was out of sight of the clinic, Zane's big hands closed around her waist and he jerked her off her feet.

Georgeanne shrieked with surprise. She was no lightweight, but Zane didn't appear to know that. No man had ever actually lifted her off her feet before. It was a novel sensation, to say the least. The next thing she knew, she lay full length on a grassy area behind the trees, with Zane stretched out beside her.

The afternoon sun behind his head cast a halo and made him look like a particularly handsome angel. The dark angel, she decided dizzily, as she stared, mesmerized, into his smoky eyes. She saw the promise of pleasure there, along with a raw, masculine power that was all too human.

His pupils had dilated and he was gazing at her in a way Georgeanne instinctively responded to. Her breathing quickened and every muscle she had tightened with excitement, because the man she desired found her desirable.

Zane gazed on her as if she was the most beautiful woman in the world. That excited her further, and she bent one knee to turn more fully toward him. Her breasts rose and fell with her rapid breathing, breathing that accelerated when he leaned toward her and cupped her chin with one hand.

"I've been wanting this for the past week," he said, "ever since I first saw you. Almost from the first letter you wrote me. Georgie, kiss me."

Georgeanne wouldn't have dreamed of not kissing him. She reached for him automatically, bringing his face down. His lips touched hers, and he made a strangled sound before his tongue thrust into her mouth, claiming her. She wrapped her arms around his neck to bring him closer during the deep, searching kiss they exchanged.

The feel of Zane's big body against hers did something to Georgeanne. She reacted in a way totally unlike herself, but she was too involved in sensation to be shocked at her own behavior. She arched her back, mutely encouraging him to explore her with his hands while he kissed her.

Zane wasted no time in answering her unspoken desire. He ran his hands down her sides then back up to cup her breasts. The wildly passionate sound she made shocked her, although it seemed to encourage Zane. He stroked his thumbs over the cloth covering her nipples and she felt them tingle with delightful sensations.

She had too many clothes on, she realized. No doctor could examine a patient who insisted upon remaining fully clothed. When Zane thrust his hands beneath the oversized blouse she wore and reached behind her for the clasp of her brassiere, she lifted to help him. The bra gave way and Zane covered her breasts with his palms.

Georgeanne gasped when she felt Zane's hands on her bare breasts. When his thumbs caressed her nipples, and his fingers joined in to learn their size and shape, she moaned aloud. He shoved her blouse up and gazed down on her, and Georgeanne recognized in his face all the emotions she experienced.

Desire this intense was foreign to her. She had never felt anything like it. She thought she was actually being drawn out of her body when she felt the warm, drawing suction of his mouth on her. The cool air on the moistened area when his mouth left one breast to taste the other created another erotic sensation that made her gasp aloud.

"You have a perfect body." Zane gazed on her with rapt attention. "I'm going to buy you one of those skimpy bikinis, and you're going to wear it. At home, for me."

Ordinarily, the thought of a bikini would have made Georgeanne think of diets and suffering. With Zane staring at her as if he couldn't get enough, she could hardly wait to put on the bikini.

"I'd love to see you in one of those thongs," she whispered.

Zane's passionate gray gaze rose to her face. "For you, I'd wear one, Georgie."

He kissed her again, teasing her mercilessly with his tongue, and then touching her breasts with little licks and nibbles. Georgeanne knew she was going out of her head. Dimly, somewhere in the back of her alleged mind, she knew that there was work to be done and that she was shirking, and that, furthermore, she was lying out in the open air letting a man who looked like a movie star undress her. *But what a way to go*, her body cried.

For once, Georgeanne was in no condition to listen to her head. She listened to her body and was lost.

Georgeanne knew something incredible was about to happen. Something she'd only dreamed about, and had once prayed to feel even a glimmering of in a man's embrace. She trembled in Zane's arms, incapable of thinking. All she could do was feel.

To her anguish, Zane stilled.

She murmured a protest and sought to pull him closer, but Zane refused to cooperate.

"Don't, Georgie. I can't wait to make love to you. But not here, and not now, where anybody could walk up on us. Someone from the clinic is liable to come looking for us at any moment."

Georgeanne's eyes flew open with dismay. She had been literally lost to the world, something that had never happened to her before. What was wrong with her?

"Besides, I don't think you're quite ready to go this far." Zane stroked her hair back from her face in a soothing motion. "I never meant to let things get out of hand like this, but you go to my head more powerfully than bourbon."

Georgeanne's thoughts tumbled through her bemused brain like pebbles in a polisher.

All these years —
So this was what —
And it hadn't been like this with —
But with Zane —
She had never wanted, never craved like —
She closed her eyes again, breaking off her disjointed thoughts. So this was the feeling she had been reaching for and couldn't find with her husband. The lack of it had destroyed Georgeanne's marriage and had caused her husband to consider her a poor excuse for a woman.

And now she had almost found out what all the fuss was about, in the arms of a man she had met barely one week ago.

Worse, if she had met Zane sooner, Fritzi Field would not currently be wreaking havoc on Georgeanne's formerly quiet life.

Georgeanne felt more convinced than ever that fate had it in for her.

Chapter 6

Zane knew he had gone too far, too fast. Georgeanne had withdrawn into her own thoughts, and those thoughts were not particularly pleasant, judging from her pensive face.

He hadn't intended to throw her down on the grass and start to make love to her while he was in the middle of cutting down a tree. Somehow, when he ran after her and caught her, it had become inevitable. Zane couldn't regret it, but he did regret causing Georgeanne distress.

He smoothed her hair back from her face and stroked his lips across her forehead. "What are you thinking, Georgie?"

She struggled to sit up and pull her blouse down in spite of Zane's heavy arm across her waist. "I was wondering what had gotten into me," she said, with the wry humor he loved in her.

Her breasts were bare to his possessive gaze. He would give almost anything to take up again right where he had left off when sanity returned.

"You're right. Anyone could walk up and see us," she added.

Georgeanne looked as though she still couldn't believe what had almost happened. Zane wondered just how extensive her experience with passion was.

He sat up beside her and helped pull her blouse down. "I know. That's why I halfway managed to keep my head. I wouldn't embarrass you like that for the world, Georgie." He reached around her to rehook her bra. "Please don't be angry with me. You're so beautiful, I couldn't resist touching you."

He found Georgeanne's passion beautiful to watch. She was completely honest, with her every emotion reflected on her face immediately. He had no doubts about the strength or the reality of her response to him. Making love to Georgeanne would be the most shattering experience of his life.

"I'm not angry, Zane." She looked away, coloring. "In fact, it… was very educational. Believe it or not, I've never understood before how a woman could let herself get carried away so completely that she finds herself pregnant." She smiled suddenly, remembered enchantment in her eyes. "Now I think I understand how it can happen."

Zane couldn't believe what he heard. He stared at Georgeanne and realized that she didn't know what she'd just told him. "I'd never put you in that position," he said roughly. "I might get carried away, but not that carried away."

"Good," she said, smiling, "because it appears that I might be somewhat lacking in willpower."

Zane quickly cupped her chin and turned her face to him. "Georgie, that's the nicest thing a woman has ever said to me. Kiss me again."

"I don't think I'd better." Her smiling brown eyes met his gaze with painful honesty. "You make me behave totally unlike myself. There's no telling what'll happen if I kiss you."

Zane had to laugh, although he could see Georgeanne still felt confused at her own response to him. "Do you think I go around tumbling women to the ground when I'm in the middle of cutting down trees for a friend?" he countered. "Georgie, what happened between us was meant to happen. I'm incredibly attracted to you. Naturally, I want to make love to you."

Georgeanne swallowed and looked away, and he hoped he saw an answering desire in her eyes before she focused her gaze on a nearby tree.

Zane chuckled again and hugged her against him. "Don't worry, Georgie. Let this be a lesson to the both of us about playing with dynamite. We'll do what one of my patients calls 'avoiding the near occasion of sin'."

Georgeanne smiled, but the smile faded.

"What's wrong, Georgie?" Zane studied her face. She was thinking about something unpleasant, something that had caused her beautiful, full mouth to tighten and her satiny skin to pale.

Georgeanne blinked. "I'm sorry. I was just…thinking. I still can't believe this happened, I suppose."

Zane threw back his head and laughed aloud. He felt exultant, as if he'd just conquered Mt. Everest or shot a canoe through dangerous white water. "Well, it did. By the way, be ready at seven tonight. I'm taking you to see Hunt's movie."

"But—"

"No buts, Georgie. You're through out here for the weekend. It's time you had a little relaxation." In her eyes, he thought he saw speculation about the natural culmination of the explosive desire between them. "Don't," he said and grinned. "I've got to get that tree down so I can feel free to enjoy myself tonight."

Georgeanne flushed. "Sorry. I was just thinking that I do feel somewhat tense. Must be the company," she added in droll tones.

"Must be." Zane rolled to his feet. If he didn't, he'd take Georgeanne up on the unconscious invitation in those dark chocolate eyes, and this time he wouldn't be able to hold himself back from making love to her.

She wasn't ready for a commitment of that magnitude, Zane realized. He already thought of her as his, and he was forgetting that Georgeanne hadn't even been on an official date with him yet. He'd better get to work to remedy that.

He stood and reached down to her, admiring her slender hands and the strong, supple body that had just moved so perfectly to his demands. Georgeanne needed a little time, and it was going to kill him to give it to her, but he'd manage somehow. He wanted her to have no regrets about the way she responded to him. If she required time to adjust, then he'd see that she got the time she needed.

"You have grass and leaves all over you." He brushed her clothes vigorously. Just touching her resurrected the desire he had managed to temporarily subdue. "Do you think anyone will know what we've been doing?"

"If I had a mirror, I could tell you," Georgeanne said with wry humor. "My face gives away everything."

"Yes," Zane said, with infinite meaning in his deep voice, "it does."

• • •

Walking beside Zane back to the clinic, Georgeanne couldn't help but notice how well their steps fit together. Zane moved with the easy stride of a man who kept his body in excellent physical condition, and with all the outdoor work and walking she did, she was in good shape as well. She never thought she would find this much enjoyment in just walking beside a man.

Georgeanne swallowed hard. If she wasn't careful, she'd fall in love with Zane Bryant. Lord knew, she was an expert at endowing a man with every virtue she wanted to see, and so far she hadn't even been forced to create any virtues for Zane. He already possessed every attribute most important to her.

Georgeanne finished out the day by attaching herself to the window trim she was painting. Her thoughts formed a peculiar morass of guilt and pleasure. Why, she asked herself, had it taken twenty-eight years for her to find a man who brought forth the response she had written about as Fritzi Field? She felt like a total fool, and she felt like kissing the world, all at the same time.

Then a peculiar thought struck: Did this mean she could now consider herself a woman? Georgeanne broke into suppressed giggles. If a woman's first sexual experience officially made her a woman, then her first real taste of sexual pleasure must make her…something.

She caught Zane's interested glance and hastily concentrated on laying paint very carefully along the window trim. Perhaps Fritzi Field's second book ought to be all about what happened inside a woman's body and mind during and after her first earth-shaking sexual experience. It would certainly be a lot more fun to research than *Faking It* had been.

Zane sent her home at five, and remembering the hot expression in his eyes brought the bright color back to her complexion. The thought of going to a movie with him placed her in yet another mental quandary.

What if Zane wanted a repeat of the afternoon's events? Realizing her body was capable of experiencing a high degree of sexual pleasure had been so shattering, she still hadn't assimilated it. Part of her wanted to run, while a greater part of her hoped Zane would kiss her like that again.

Just the thought of what had almost happened between them made Georgeanne feel weak. She drove down the long, narrow road toward her isolated country house and relived the experience. She was lucky she didn't drive off the road.

Her two dogs appeared when she pulled into the circular drive before her house. Georgeanne stared at the scene, trying to see it through Zane's eyes, and decided it was impossible. A man either loved country living or he didn't.

Her husband hadn't, but Georgeanne had steadfastly refused to sell the house that was her only legacy from parents who had died when Georgeanne was ten. Her grandfather had farmed rice and raised cattle on the surrounding fields for nearly fifty years, but the house and two acres were all that remained of those many acres of land. Georgeanne considered the house her heritage, which would belong someday to her children. If she ever had any.

"Love me, love my house and dogs," Georgeanne muttered, climbing out of her SUV.

She stood a moment gazing at the white farm house. Spring had brought out the honeysuckle and trumpet vine that screened the front porch. The two sycamore trees her grandfather had planted were fresh with spring-green foliage. The wooden farmhouse had a lot of charm, thanks to Georgeanne's careful planting and tending of shrubs.

The dogs had ruined her efforts to nurture a flower garden, but Georgeanne didn't mind. Not when they came rushing up to her every evening full of joyous welcome.

Roscoe was a medium-sized long-haired dog whose parentage likely included English setter and fox terrier, and his buddy, Jack, combined several varieties of terrier in a facade that only a mother could love. Although Georgeanne wasn't Jack's mother, she did love him, and both dogs gave her all the love and protection a woman who lived alone in the country could want.

She bestowed rubs and fond words impartially on the two happy dogs and unlocked the front door. The insistent ringing of the telephone met her ears. Georgeanne hurried to answer it. Perhaps Zane was calling to cancel their date.

Then she recalled that Zane had her cell phone number. That meant only one thing.

"Hi, kid. It's about time you got home," her agent, Alice Anson, said in her trumpeting voice.

Georgeanne suppressed a groan. Of all the awful times for Alice to call, this had to be the worst.

"Hi, Alice," she returned, with a pronounced lack of enthusiasm. "This is Sunday. Don't you ever take a day off?"

"Are you kidding? I'm a literary agent." Alice's familiar, rasping voice was laced with humor. "When do you think I get any reading done? Look, Georgie, we could be making a mint off this book of yours. When are you going to do everyone a favor and accept some of these talk show invitations? I've had at least ten calls these last two days—"

"Never," Georgeanne yelped. "Alice, I will not change my mind. Don't ask me again."

"You're sounding hysterical, kid. What's up?"

"I'll tell you what's up. One of my friends at work is carting a copy of the book around and is reading excerpts aloud. I'm going nuts, that's what's up. Why would I want to go on a talk show and talk still more about that stupid book?"

"Don't insult our product." Alice's voice took on a soothing quality. "That book is a beautiful little money-maker, and don't you forget it. I worked on that package."

"I know." Instantly remorseful, Georgeanne collapsed on the sofa. "So did I. The thing is, I never expected it to be such a hit."

"I told you it would." Alice's voice became reasonable. "Why do you think I took it on? I don't represent just any manuscript, you know. A work has to move me in a really big way before I'll waste my valuable time on it."

Georgeanne, as always, began to feel guilty about robbing poor Alice of money the agent had earned fair and square in spite of the fact that, in reality, Alice worked for her. "I appreciate all your hard work, Alice, but the truth is, I'm a very private person. If you want to hire an actress to be Fritzi Field, believe me, I'll understand."

"Kid, the only person who can do this book justice is the author, and don't you forget it. The issues it raises come from the heart and soul of a real woman. Just think about how many more copies your personal appearances will sell. That's all I ask. Just think about it. And think about quitting that dinky job of yours while you're at it. Now's the time to write a follow-up to *Faking It.* And you could use a Facebook page and a website, not to mention a Twitter account and something on Pinterest. Think of the followers you'd have. Think of the increased sales."

Georgeanne thought about it for one-tenth of a second. This time she did moan aloud. "I'm sorry, Alice. I just don't have anything further to say on the subject."

"That'll change," Alice predicted. "Your publisher has collected up quite a bit of mail for Fritzi Field. They packed it up a few days ago and mailed out to you. Once you start reading it, you'll realize you owe the public another book, not to mention access to the author." There was a silence, as if Alice was refreshing herself from the ubiquitous cup of coffee on her desk. "The readers are full of questions. You'll find yourself writing two or three books just to get them all answered."

"I don't know, Alice." Two more books on faking orgasm? No way. "Writing the last one really took it out of me."

"Wait till your royalty check arrives," Alice said in soothing tones. "You'll feel much better right away, believe me."

Georgeanne replaced the receiver. She would not feel better about it. She would never feel better about it, no matter how many clinics the money would fund, or how much dog food she could buy for the Humane Society. She'd like to pack the royalty check, the letters, and anything else identifying her as Fritzi Field and ship them all back to New York.

Someone knocked at the door. Georgeanne looked out and saw a brown delivery truck sitting in her driveway being checked out by her dogs.

"Two packages for Miss Georgeanne Hartfield," the man said.

Georgeanne looked down. The delivery dolly held two large cardboard boxes bearing the logo of her publisher. She couldn't believe it. Two big boxes full of letters for Fritzi Field? When was she supposed to get time to read them all?

She had the postman unload the boxes just inside her living room door, intending to carry them to her bedroom and stuff them out of sight in her closet, but the doorbell rang again before the mail truck had exited her driveway.

The dogs didn't bark. That meant a friend. Georgeanne opened the door with a feeling of impending doom.

"Georgie," Denise Devereaux said, "I mean it. I want you to read this book. I need someone like Fritzi to talk to about it."

Georgeanne suppressed an urge to deny all interest in Fritzi Field's theories. "I'm awfully busy right now…"

"I know." Denise shoved a copy of *Faking It* into Georgeanne's hands. "You've got a date with Zane Bryant, right? The man has great taste. I will say that for him."

Georgeanne, constitutionally incapable of saying no to her friends, resigned herself to a few nights devoted to Fritzi Field. "All right, Denise. I'll read it."

Denise's lovely face glowed with gratitude. "I've marked the parts I want you to pay particular attention to. That's your own copy, by the way. I can't give mine up."

Georgeanne looked down at the book in her hands with an inward shudder. Her author's copies lay safely hidden on the top shelf of her linen closet. Her pride in her accomplishment had lasted all of nine months, until the day she'd seen a display of the books in a local bookstore that had already been depleted by customers. She'd known then that her quiet, anonymous life in the country was in jeopardy.

"I'll do my best." Georgeanne just hoped she could come up with a reasonable analysis of the book. How did one analyze her own work without dithering around like a complete idiot?

"I've decided to start a website devoted to *Faking It*." Denise's normally dignified face now held the ardent look of a crusader. "If no one around here feels the way I do, I'll connect with some people online. I just know there are more women out there who love this book. Maybe we can get Fritzi to talk to us online."

Georgeanne made a sound that even she recognized as something similar to the wheeze made by a dying duck.

"In the meantime," Denise added, "your job is to read that book and let me ask you lots of questions." Her gaze fell on the two newly delivered boxes. "Need some help moving those?"

"I'm keeping them for a friend," Georgeanne thought Denise regarded the boxes a little too closely. "I'll see if I can get the first few chapters read this weekend."

Georgeanne shut the door behind Denise and gave the book a glance of loathing. At least she didn't have to actually read it in order to know what it said. But a website? Maybe she'd better read the book in hopes that Denise's urge to seek out other devotees to *Faking It* would be assuaged before she started the website.

She glanced toward the kitchen, saw the time, and gave a small shriek. Zane was due in fifteen minutes, and she wasn't even dressed. Her hair was hopeless. Thank goodness she had perfected a system years ago for days like this.

The system worked so well that she went warm all over when she opened her front door and Zane's appreciative gaze rested on her.

"Georgie, you look more beautiful than ever," he said. "I can see I wasted my time feeling guilty about the fact that I gave you so little time to get ready."

Georgeanne had pulled her heavy mass of brown hair smoothly back from her forehead and had secured it at the top of her head with an ornamental clip. Then she simply let it tumble down to join the rest of her hair, and it didn't matter so much that most of the curl had fallen out of it.

She wore a simple dress of emerald knitted fabric that skimmed her figure and made the most of every curve she had. Men always turned to look at her in that dress as if they actually preferred a woman with curves.

Judging from the expression on his lean, handsome face and lurking in his eyes, Zane liked her curves. Georgeanne's spirits, temporarily depressed from excessive contact with Fritzi Field's affairs, lifted immeasurably.

Her dogs sniffed cautiously at Zane's heels as he stepped across the threshold. "How long will it be until they decide I'm a friend?" Zane stepped inside at her invitation and his gaze fell upon the two boxes she hadn't yet moved. "Need some help with those?"

Georgeanne paled and mentally cursed herself for the way her ridiculous complexion insisted upon behaving. "Leave them there, please. I still have to decide where I want to put them. Would you like something to drink?"

"Better not. We barely have time to make the show." Zane stared around the room. "This is a beautiful place. It feels like home."

Georgeanne looked around at her comfortable, country-style furniture and the light, airy quality she had achieved with sheer curtains and cream-colored walls. She loved the plain and simple and felt inordinately pleased that Zane apparently did, too.

Too late, Georgeanne realized she had laid Denise's book on an end table. Zane picked it up. Her heart sank when his gaze went swiftly from the logo on the boxes to the matching publisher's imprint on the book jacket.

He turned the book in his big hands, studying the rave reviews decorating the back cover. "I see you broke down and bought a copy."

Conscious of the absurd flushing of her skin, Georgeanne strove to concentrate on picking up her purse. "Denise bought me a copy. She wants me to read it and give her a report."

"I see." Zane thumbed lightly through the book. "She seems to have marked several places she wants you to pay special attention to."

He opened the book to the foreword and skimmed it. Georgeanne felt sure he had mastered the entire contents of the foreword within the few seconds he spent reading it. He closed the book at last and laid it down. His penetrating gray gaze created extreme discomfort in Georgeanne's psyche.

"Interesting," he said. "I'll definitely have to buy myself a copy. The author claims she wrote the book to save marriages."

Georgeanne swallowed hard, but her throat was too dry for speech. She wasn't at all sure she wanted to know what Zane thought of the book, but the downfall of an author was ever curiosity about what readers thought of her work.

"What did you think of the foreword?" she asked, then added hastily, "I haven't read it yet, but Sandra and Denise were...quite impressed by it." She reddened involuntarily.

Zane smiled, gray eyes warming when they rested on her. "I can see why. The author has the ability to convey honesty and caring without sentimentality. If the rest of the book reads like the foreword, this is an intensely personal book. The author probably wrote it on the strength of her own experience and convictions."

Georgeanne experienced a sinking feeling. Perhaps she was suffering a belated crisis over the fact that readers actually recognized the personal nature of the book.

"We were wondering at the office if a man could possibly have written it," she said. "Say, a doctor with a lot of anatomical experience."

Zane grinned. "Is that right? I understand there are some graphic descriptions of female sexual response. Anyone with sufficient education could probably research whatever they needed."

That was exactly what Georgeanne had done, even going so far as to request interlibrary loans. What if the head librarian read *Faking It* and remembered one Georgeanne Hartfield's preoccupation with that very subject about two years ago? Georgeanne's infamous complexion promptly paled.

Zane stepped closer. "Georgie, what is it? You look like you're about to faint."

"It's just my habit of registering every stray thought on my skin." Georgeanne turned toward the door. "All my life, people have wondered what embarrassed me or what was about to make me faint. Ignore it, Zane. It's a simple constriction or dilation of the arteries near my skin's surface. It may or may not have anything to do with what I'm thinking."

Zane studied her face but said nothing more. He helped her into his car to the accompaniment of further inspection by her dogs, made a couple of good-natured remarks to the dogs, and came around. "This place has the loving look of an old family homestead. Was it handed down to you, by any chance?"

"As a matter of fact, it was," Georgeanne said, surprised at his insight. "My grandparents used to farm rice on the land as far away as you can see in all directions. When my parents died, my grandfather left it to me."

"How old were you when your parents died?" Zane held out his hand.

Georgeanne automatically placed her hand in his. "I was ten." She forced a smile. "My father's brother took me to live with him and his wife in Shreveport. They were very good to me."

"But?" Zane asked, as if certain there was a "but" somewhere.

Georgeanne reminded herself that Zane was a pediatrician accustomed to obtaining information from his little patients by using the sixth sense many doctors had lost with the advent of blood tests and modern machinery. "They had expected to have children of their own. When that didn't happen, they jumped at the chance to take me, but my poor aunt didn't know what to do with a child like me."

"What do you mean, Georgie?" Zane studied her face thoughtfully while he started his car. "You don't strike me as the sort of person who had a troublesome childhood."

"Oh, no," she assured him hastily. "I went out of my way to avoid causing my aunt and uncle any trouble." How could she explain the real trouble, which was that her height and intelligence had been an embarrassment to her aunt? "It's just that I wasn't the sort of child my aunt had in mind when my uncle brought me home to her."

"What sort of child did she have in mind?" Zane looked at her as if he couldn't imagine any adult not appreciating Georgeanne as a child.

"She had hoped I'd be a cute little thing who would grow up to be popular and sought-after," Georgeanne said in a rush. "Instead, I was shy and quiet and bookish. On top of that, I was taller than every boy in class. She didn't know how to dress me, or even how to talk to me. I was a great disappointment to her."

"If she was expecting to live her life through you, I should hope she was," Zane said. "Every child is an individual."

"They did their best." Georgeanne overall considered herself lucky in life. "They gave me a good home and a good education, and—" She broke off before she could say, "a big wedding." Her aunt had been thrilled about her marriage to Tony Rollins, and Georgeanne preferred not to think or talk about her marriage. "For the most part, I had a happy, normal childhood and a lot of good friends."

• • •

Zane heard Georgeanne's unspoken words almost as unerringly as if she had said them aloud. Dr. Gant had been a regular fount of disgust when it came to describing Tony Rollins. Zane had formed the image of a man too strikingly handsome for his own good, a spoiled boy who had taken one look at Georgeanne Hartfield and had grabbed for her and all she represented.

If Georgeanne had spent much of her childhood disappointing her aunt, she must have jumped at the chance to please her when Tony Rollins appeared. That explained why Georgeanne had married a man who had obviously never bothered to please her in any way.

Feeling as if he understood Georgeanne much better, Zane told her about his adoptive parents, who were alive and well in Dallas, and who had unofficially adopted Hunter Howell the day Zane had brought him home for the first time.

"I'll always wonder what our lives would have been like if Hunt had grown up with me in my parents' home," he finished. "He's a wary sort, but he warmed to them at once. They have a knack for taking in strays." He smiled at her. "Rather like you, Georgie."

"I hope they have a big yard and lots of money for dog or cat food," Georgeanne said, in humorous tones. "When you have a knack like that, you'd better have the income to support it."

"My dad's a doctor. Like me, he'll never be a particularly rich doctor, but he makes a good living. My mother was a nurse, but she stopped working when they adopted me."

"They sound like wonderful people," Georgeanne said and smiled. "Maybe it's a good thing you and Hunter didn't grow up as brothers. Together, you might have been holy terrors."

Zane turned the car in at a movie theater and parked. "In about an hour and a half, you can reassess that statement." He smiled tenderly at her, well aware that her light tone covered deep emotion. "You could be right. There's something about having company in deviltry that encourages boys to outdo themselves."

Inside the darkened theater, Zane held Georgeanne's hand and made himself comfortable in a position where he could watch her expressive face. He never tired of watching the constant fluctuations of color in her cheeks, or the way her dark eyes widened or narrowed with her emotions.

Her hand rested in his, and he stroked his fingers over the elegant bones of her wrists and fingers. She wasn't used to having her hand held in a movie, but she adapted well. He fed her popcorn and enjoyed himself watching her face while she experienced the events of the movie along with Hunter Howell.

Zane gave a passing glance at Hunter onscreen. He'd seen the movie a couple of times already, and each time he'd felt as though he was watching himself. He just hoped no one in the theater got the idea that he was Hunter Howell and ruined his first date with Georgeanne. He had forgotten the dark glasses he usually brought along for occasions like this.

He watched Georgeanne follow the movie events and enjoyed the feel of her hand clasped in his. Her hand had been made to fit his, he decided, just as her body fit his to perfection.

As if she detected his thoughts, Georgeanne reddened, but she never took her eyes from the screen. Perhaps the movie love scene called the afternoon's events to her mind.

The movie had a simple plot wherein Hunter Howell, hardened police detective, fell in love with the battered society wife he was assigned to protect and ended up killing her husband. Then Hunter took the woman he had fallen in love with to bed.

Georgeanne stared at the screen and audibly sucked in her breath, clearly experiencing the emotions of the two lovers.

Zane grinned into the darkness that fell over the theater while the couple interacted beneath the sheets. "Careful, Georgie," he whispered in her ear. "You're about to crush my fingers."

Chapter 7

"Well?" Zane stuck his spoon into the banana split beside Georgeanne's spoon. "What did you think?"

Georgeanne was still too shaken from her own thoughts during the movie's single, well-choreographed love scene to reply with much sense. She felt Zane's intense gaze on her face and pretended great interest in the ice cream.

"I can see why his acting career took off. He's…very good."

Zane hadn't said anything else about the way she'd squeezed his hand during the love scene, but Georgeanne knew he understood exactly what her thoughts had been. He had remained blessedly silent on the subject while they drove to the ice cream shop.

"Now, Georgie, I'm a doctor of little kids. Don't you think I know an evasion when I hear one?" He smiled and watched the color rise in Georgeanne's cheeks.

"I—" Georgeanne abruptly gave up pretending she was a sophisticated woman of the world. "Zane, the truth is, he's so much like you, it makes me want to cry. But he also reminds me of a child who's been beaten one too many times."

Zane's steady gaze held hers. "Yes. Go on, please."

"There's no way anyone can get behind that facade of his without a crowbar." Georgeanne drew in a deep breath. "Even while—even during the love scene, I kept feeling that he was hiding his real emotions behind what he imagined people expected to see. And he did a good job of it. For a minute there, I almost thought—that is, I could almost imagine…"

She trailed off. For a moment, she'd been able to enter fully into the imaginary world of the pictured love scene because Zane had been looking out of his twin's eyes. Then the long dark lashes had swept down. When they lifted again, Hunter Howell was back, a man who had learned early that the only person he could count on was himself. She didn't need to be told that he kept the part of himself that was like Zane very carefully hidden.

Georgeanne sighed and concentrated on the ice cream. There she went again, psychoanalyzing a man she had never met. If ever anyone was unqualified to analyze another person, it had to be Georgeanne Hartfield.

"That's amazing," Zane said. "Dr. Baghri was right about you."

"No, he wasn't." She looked up and laughed. "That is, I don't know what he told you, but I'm sure it's untrue."

"He said you have what the country people in America call the second sight. You see into the heart of a person."

Georgeanne kept her gaze focused on the ice cream. "Now, Zane, how can I possibly see into someone's heart when he's an actor on a movie screen? I'm probably looking at him and seeing you. It's amazing how physically alike the two of you are."

"I should have worn sunglasses," Zane said in resigned tones. "I'm not used to life as a celebrity."

"Well, naturally people coming out of a movie that starred Hunter Howell are going to think you're him." She glanced around the small ice cream parlor, relieved to note that they were the only customers at the moment. "And just as naturally, they're going to hope you're lying when you claim you aren't Hunter Howell."

Zane scowled. Georgeanne noted that his good looks were unblemished by the scowl.

"Hunt is going to have to do something about this," he said.

"Have you told him so?"

"As a matter of fact, I have." Zane eyed her smiling face with mock annoyance. "He laughed."

Zane sounded so injured, Georgeanne couldn't resist a chuckle. "I imagine he'll do interviews in which he tells everybody to leave his brother, the doctor, alone. He should enjoy that considerably."

"You see? I knew you had his number." Zane grinned at her.

"It isn't hard to draw the conclusion that if he'd had the opportunity, he'd be a doctor rather than a movie star, no matter how big his career might get." Georgeanne looked down at their side-by-side spoons. There was something cozy about sharing a banana split with Zane. "I don't think he really likes being well-known. To him, stardom is probably a means to an end."

Zane watched her with his intense doctor's gaze. "What do you think Hunter's 'end' is?"

Georgeanne thought a moment. Impressions about Hunter Howell poured into her brain and she sorted them out. During the movie, she'd been so busy thinking how like Zane he was, she hadn't consciously noted any personality quirks.

"I think Hunter is probably interested in...Well, judging strictly from what you've told me of his background, I'd say he's interested in something to do with foster care. Or adoption follow-ups." She made a motion of dismissal with her hands, suddenly embarrassed. Not even full-fledged psychiatrists had any right to go around making assumptions about people they'd never met. Since Georgeanne had never practiced as a psychologist, she was particularly sensitive about attempting to analyze people. "But I'm probably all wrong. Maybe he's interested in homes for unwed mothers."

Zane threw back his head and laughed, obviously delighted. "Georgie, you've done it again. You know him better than I do. I'd never have guessed all that about him after watching one movie." He laughed some more. "You even picked up on the homes for unwed mothers. No one but us knows that, so for God's sake, don't say a word. Hunt would kill me."

Georgeanne blinked, surprised. Maybe she did have some form of ESP, although she preferred to think of it as educated guesswork. "Now, Zane, I had the advantage of knowing you, and of knowing a few facts about identical twins. I told you, they tend to grow remarkably alike no matter what their individual upbringings."

Zane leaned back and smiled at her. "Tell me something personal, Georgie. Why are you running around alone and unattached?"

"I'm a divorced woman, and a very busy one. It's only when a man intrudes face first into my world that I sit up and take notice."

"Thank God you've put away the blue toys," Zane said, laughing again. "I don't want any other men entering your life face first. What are you doing tomorrow after work? Besides reading Fritzi Field's book," he added.

Georgeanne propped her chin on her hand and pretended intense thought. It wasn't easy, now that Fritzi Field had reentered her mind. "I'll probably go by the clinic and make sure the new telephone system is working. The phone company supposed to be out bright and early Monday morning."

He smiled. "Dr. Baghri approves of my new interest, by the way. I believe he assumes you're spending all this time educating me about his clinic idea."

Georgeanne chuckled. "I should probably be feeling guilty for distracting you. It was inadvertent, I assure you."

"Georgie, you're the best thing that's ever happened to me. I had given up on finding a truly honest woman."

Georgeanne swallowed a bite of ice cream the wrong way and coughed violently for a few minutes.

"Are you all right?" Zane watched her with concern. "Do I need to perform the Heimlich maneuver or something?"

"Not on ice cream that went down the wrong way," Georgeanne managed. "It was the shock of hearing you describe me as a truly honest woman that did it. Where on earth did you get that idea?"

Zane leaned forward. "Your face. Any lie you told would be instantly visible to anyone who isn't blind."

"Oh." Georgeanne considered investing heavily in makeup. An inch deep on the foundation might do the trick. "Well. I'm glad to know that."

"Come on, Georgie. You look like you sat on an ant bed. What is it you're hiding? Confess."

She met his gaze in one startled glance, and then looked down. "If I'm hiding something, you'll have to find a way to pry it out of me. And I'm invulnerable to tickling, I might add."

"Is that right?" Zane laughed, clearly delighted. "The last person who told me that turned out to be the most ticklish person in the universe."

Georgeanne eyed him reproachfully.

"Besides, there are better ways than tickling to get information out of you," he went on.

"No, there aren't. I mean—" Georgeanne stabbed the banana split with her spoon. "How did we get into this conversation?"

"Ah-ha. I was right." Zane pretended to twirl an imaginary mustache. "You are ticklish. But don't worry, Georgie. When I'm ready to hear the truth from you, I'll just find a grassy nook and kiss you into submission. Something tells me you'd sing a lot faster."

Georgeanne smiled, a purely feminine smile. "I probably would. When I'm tickled, all I do is scream bloody murder."

Zane stared at her. "I'll remember that."

Two women entered the shop, chatting energetically.

"Her husband dumped her," one said. "I knew it the minute I read the first paragraph. Why else would a woman think faking it was the only way to go?"

Georgeanne's head came up like a startled deer's, and she knew she must resemble a doe facing a shotgun.

"Wait till you read the tenth chapter," the other woman said. "That's where she goes into detail about the physical signs. Can you believe anyone would go through that much trouble just to hold on to a man?"

"Beats me. I don't have trouble with that sort of thing."

Georgeanne smiled involuntarily. Then she realized what she was doing and strove to wipe all expression off her face. If Zane were to read the passage in Fritzi Field's book that dealt with modern women's compulsion to pretend they enjoyed every sexual encounter, he would have to realize she knew a lot more about Fritzi Field's book than she let on.

"Neither do I," the first woman said. "That book is nothing but a commercial plot. You can mark my words."

The two women reached the counter and ceased talking to concentrate on which ice cream to order.

"Georgie, you look like someone's holding a knife to your throat," Zane said. "What is it about Fritzi Field's book that scares you so badly?"

"Scares me?" Georgeanne repeated faintly. "Nothing about it scares me, except the fact that Denise wants me to read it, preferably tonight."

"I suppose that's enough to scare anybody." Zane was silent a moment, studying her face as she focused on the ice cream. "Georgie, what's your opinion of women who fake sexual enjoyment?"

Her gaze lifted to meet his. "I haven't formed an opinion yet. Wait until I read the book. Fritzi Field might succeed in giving me a whole new outlook on the subject."

"I gather Denise Devereaux has gained a whole new outlook already," Zane said.

Georgeanne noted the austere note in Zane's voice and shivered. Of course, he was a man, and no sane man would approve of a woman who had to put on an act in order to keep her husband. What man would like to think his woman was faking enjoyment of his caresses?

If Zane should ever realize who wrote *Faking It*, anything between them would be over. Her every response to him would be suspect. Why would he believe her when she swore he was the only man ever to evoke such a response from her?

"You're right. Denise has formed a whole new opinion of the subject," Georgeanne said, in faint tones. "That's why she wants me to read the book. I think she's hoping I'll agree with her that a woman has a right to do whatever is necessary in order to save her marriage."

"Georgie, are you sure you're all right? You look like you're about to faint again."

"I'm fine. Just fine." Georgeanne swallowed and strove for control. "Don't pay any attention to my complexion. It has a life of its own, believe me." She might as well know the worst at once. It was obvious she was going to be up all night doing some heavy thinking. "What do you think, Zane? About women who fake sexual enjoyment, I mean."

Zane watched her face closely. She hoped he saw nothing in her expression to arouse his suspicions, but she feared he might.

"I don't think you need to worry about my opinion of that, Georgie," he said. "It's obvious enough that there's a lot of chemistry between us. When we make love, you're going to enjoy it as much as I will, never doubt it."

Georgeanne noted his use of "when" rather than "if," and tried to ignore her doubts. Just because she felt things so intensely when Zane kissed her didn't necessarily mean she was capable of experiencing full sexual pleasure.

"I gather you don't approve," she said. "Being a man, I don't suppose you would."

Zane shook his head. "Two people ought not get married if there's no sexual excitement between them. One or the other is bound to feel cheated."

"You're right, of course."

She said nothing more. No one agreed with that statement more thoroughly than the author of *Faking It,* but Georgeanne knew now was not the time to bring up the question of women who found themselves in a marriage where lack of sexual enjoyment on their part was one of the major items plaguing their marriages. Zane would simply reply that said women should have known better than to marry men they felt no physical response toward.

"Somehow, I can't imagine you ever doing such a thing, Georgie," Zane said. "You're much too honest, for one thing. For another, you have such a passionate nature."

Georgeanne gulped and spoke a thought that was new to her. "I think the degree of passion in a relationship depends on the man a woman is with."

The realization stunned Georgeanne. She had been married to the wrong man, and she hadn't even realized it. She had thought all the problems in her marriage were her fault. She had thought a woman was supposed to feel sexual enjoyment the way a man did. A few minutes lying in the grass with Zane Bryant had showed her that, for her at least, sexual enjoyment was based on something more than the promise of simple physical release.

Her head whirled. She'd have to think this one out. Could it be that all the clichés about meeting "Mr. Right" weren't clichés at all, but a basic truth?

Zane stretched out one big hand across the table toward her. "Georgie, that's the second nicest thing any woman has ever said to me."

Stunned, Georgeanne looked blankly at him a moment before placing her hand in his. If Zane Bryant was her own Mr. Right, then she was in very, very deep trouble.

• • •

Georgeanne's tentative, unmentioned-even-to-herself hope that Zane would kiss her the way he had earlier came to naught. By the time he drove her home and sat down on her comfortable sofa for a cup of coffee, Zane's answering service rang his cell phone with an urgent message.

Zane answered the call, then kissed Georgeanne hurriedly and left. One of his young patients had landed in the hospital emergency ward, and was hysterically demanding Zane rather than any other doctor. Because Zane was the type of man he was, he left at once rather than insist that the child submit to another physician.

Georgeanne registered that, even as she admitted to herself that she felt relieved to have the matter taken out of her hands for the night.

She ignored the swelling disappointment in her heart. Making love with Zane just to test her new thoughts on sexual pleasure would be a big mistake on her part. She wasn't a woman who could indulge unscathed in affairs. If she made love with a man, it meant she planned on marrying him.

That naturally led Georgeanne to ask herself why she had let Zane touch her so intimately that afternoon. Never in her life had she known such desire to feel a man's hands on her bare skin. Why had it happened like that with Zane so soon after she'd met him, and never with her husband during two years of marriage?

Georgeanne shied away from answering her own question. The only answer that came to her was too shattering to contemplate. Instead, she decided that there was something basically unfair about the whole idea of a Mr. Right.

She went to bed in the middle of an argument with herself, but the only conclusion she reached was that the concept of a Mr. Right had nothing to do with a man's looks. Tony Rollins was movie-star handsome. She had thought him incredibly good-looking, but she hadn't wanted him to touch her intimately. In fact, most of his attraction for her had lain in the fact that her aunt was so thrilled at his preference for Georgeanne.

Georgeanne lay in bed staring out the moonlit window as she tried to work through the morass of her own thoughts. Outside, the leaves of the redbud tree formed dark silhouettes against the paler night sky, and Georgeanne fancied she saw Zane's profile among them. That led to remembering how his lips had felt on her breasts, and the way his long, thick lashes had brushed her neck.

The telephone rang, and Georgeanne fairly pounced on the extension beside her bed. Anything to keep from thinking.

"No, Denise, I haven't finished reading it yet," she said.

"Didn't you at least read the foreword?" Zane Bryant asked, sounding amused.

"Zane?" Surprise suspended her voice for a moment.

"Definitely, I'm buying a copy of that book," Zane said. "If Denise is so determined for you to read it, she's taken to calling you at midnight..."

"Well, she does seem rather determined that I get busy on it right away. She's already called me twice tonight." She collected her thoughts. "How was the little boy?"

"He's going to be fine," Zane said. "It was a case of asthma brought on by a rough afternoon session with the family dog. A day in the hospital and he'll be fine."

"I hope you aren't going to tell the family to get rid of the family dog." Georgeanne lay back against her pillow.

"I wouldn't dream of it, although I did tell his mother to stop smoking in the house. Georgie, I'm sorry I had to leave so suddenly. This isn't the way I planned the weekend."

She chuckled. "I've been working for doctors for the past two years. Believe me, I know how these things operate. A doctor's time is not his own, even when he isn't on call."

"Most women aren't as understanding as you are." Zane sighed. "I'm on call next weekend. I'll have to miss the dedication ceremony."

Georgeanne suppressed a sigh of her own. "That's too bad. You'll miss Dr. Baghri's speech, the one I spent all day Friday typing."

Zane laughed. "The one you wrote, you mean."

They talked a while longer about Zane's work and her own. Georgeanne hung up with a lighter heart. Zane was interested in her. No man called a woman at midnight just to talk unless he wanted to see her again.

Her heart plummeted. If Zane found out who Fritzi Field really was …

Why should he, her mind argued. Alice wouldn't betray her. Surely the public wasn't interested enough in a lone pop psychologist's view of sex and marriage to send out investigative reporters in search of the real Fritzi Field. The book simply wasn't that important. Soon, it would fade from public interest.

But not right away, she discovered. Monday morning. Denise was lying in wait for her when Georgeanne arrived at the Gant Clinic.

"Did you finish reading it?"

Georgeanne had spent a few moments that morning reviewing *Faking It* and thought she had worked out a strategy. "Yes, I read it. It was a fast read, however, so don't count too much on my opinion."

"I understand." Denise grabbed Georgeanne's arm. "You can formulate your professional opinion later. Just step right this way and tell me all about your off-the-cuff opinion."

Georgeanne obligingly let herself be herded into Dr. Gant's office. "Believe it or not, my opinion won't take too terribly long to deliver." She plucked the book from her canvas briefcase, relieved to be rid of it, and handed it to Denise, who received it with a reverence that made its author distinctly uncomfortable. "Let's lend this copy to Sandra."

"I'll give it to her in a few minutes. Now all I want is your true, unvarnished opinion of what the woman says." Denise shut the office door. "Talk, Georgie."

"Well, the first thing that impressed me was how bitter she sounds," Georgeanne said.

It had been a shock to reread parts of *Faking It*. Georgeanne reflected that if she'd put the manuscript aside a few weeks and then reread it before querying agents, she'd probably have given the book the deep-six treatment. She regarded the tome in Denise's arms with something akin to loathing.

"Well, I, for one, couldn't blame her." Denise perched on the edge of Dr. Gant's desk and regarded Georgeanne with intensity. "The fact is, she would never have written this book if she hadn't been bitter, and if she hadn't had the strength and intelligence to look back and see her own mistakes. Now go on, Georgie."

Nonplussed, Georgeanne sought for words. "You certainly don't want to base any of your own actions on a book based on bitterness and anger without thinking it over carefully."

"I don't think the things Fritzi advocates in her book are necessarily based on bitterness or anger," Denise countered. "My feeling was that she sort of went off and licked her wounds when her marriage ended, and this was what occurred to her."

Georgeanne gulped. Denise had no idea how accurate that statement was.

"She believes that if she'd had this knowledge during her marriage, she'd still be married," Denise continued.

"The question is, would that be what she really wants today?" Georgeanne asked quietly. "Now that her marriage is over, Fritzi is free to find a man who does make her heart beat faster, and whose lovemaking would cause her to feel all those things she wasn't feeling during her marriage."

Georgeanne had a strange feeling that she was not the person saying these words. They poured out of her, and she felt as if she was listening to the thoughts for the first time.

When she heard her own words, she knew this was the realization she'd been waiting for, the key idea that an entire new way of thinking would be based upon. Zane Bryant had been the catalyst that crystallized the idea—for every woman there existed a man whose touch could make her forget the world around her.

Or maybe he was the creator of the entire idea, Georgeanne thought wryly. Such an idea had never crossed her mind before without being followed immediately by the thought that such a man obviously didn't exist for her. She had gotten to where she had refused to even entertain such a thought any longer.

"That may not be possible," Denise said, in such positive tones, Georgeanne had a peculiar sense of *deja vu*. "What if you're a person who just doesn't…feel all that stuff during sex that everyone else is claiming they feel?"

Georgeanne took a moment to answer. It was a surprise to learn that Denise, of all people, had felt exactly as she had felt when her marriage ended—that something was wrong with her.

Denise went on, "Don't you remember how hard you and I laughed over the way women these days are so careful to make sure everyone knows they have no trouble reaching orgasm? Well, when I read a passage about that very phenomenon in Fritzi's book, I knew I had found another kindred spirit. You have no idea what this book has meant to me." She clutched the book against her starched white cotton-covered breasts.

Georgeanne winced. "Denise, believe me when I say you just haven't met the right man yet. As beautiful as you are—"

Denise's face took on a sardonic expression. "Now, Georgie, you sound just like my mama."

Georgeanne laughed. "This is between you and me. When my divorce became final, I felt exactly the way you feel right now. Sex was one of the biggest problems my husband and I had. It wasn't the only problem, but it seemed to me to be the biggest. Anyway, if I'd read Fritzi Field's book before my divorce, I might have made a terrible mistake. What if I'd put into practice the ideas she gives, and kept my marriage alive?"

Denise tilted her head to the side and studied her friend. "Do you know, I've always suspected your marriage ended for the same reason mine did. You always looked so peculiar every time we spoke of Fritzi Field's book, I knew there was something behind it."

"Can you blame me?" Georgeanne moved toward the door. "But this past week, I've met someone who—who—"

She couldn't go on, since she didn't know how to tell Denise that Zane Bryant made her feel the way Tony Rollins never had.

"Who makes you feel all warm and womanly?" Denise knew anyway.

"That's right." Georgeanne let her breath out. "I realized last night that I should never have married Tony. I never felt about him the way I now know I should have before I married him. His kisses left me cold. There's no other way to say it."

Denise studied her face. "Georgie, that's all very well when there aren't any children involved. It's easy to just pull up stakes and move on."

"You don't have any children." Georgeanne knew what was coming, but that didn't stop her from trying to head it off.

"What if I had? Children are damaged by divorce," Denise announced. "No one wants to admit it, including all the psychologists who have been advising everyone to please themselves and to heck with self-sacrifice."

"We're talking about you and me. Neither of us has any children that need to be considered."

"Well, Fritzi Field considered the children. I'm telling you, Georgie, that woman knows the score and she doesn't mind laying it on you. I agree with her. If a pretense of sexual enjoyment is all it takes to keep a husband and wife together long enough to get the kids raised, then whose business is it?"

Georgeanne tried for dignity as she edged once more toward the door. "If children are involved, and lack of sexual enjoyment is the chief impediment to a happy marriage, then maybe Fritzi Field is right. Maybe saving the marriage in a case like that would be worthwhile. But—"

"Come on, Georgie." Denise tapped her perfectly manicured nails on the book. "Look at what it's like out there now for a single woman. What with all the possible diseases, I'm scared to death to kiss a man, and that's assuming I can find one who's worth kissing. Now don't you think it would be better to hold onto your husband rather than try to find another man these days?"

"What would life be without something to strive for and to look forward to?" A purely female smile curved Georgeanne's lips as she opened the office door. "Especially when you consider the delights in store for you if you happen to find your Mr. Right."

Chapter 8

Georgeanne peeked into the examining room of the newly operational Saturday Children's Clinic and experienced a peculiar fluttering of her heart. Perhaps she was developing an arrhythmia. She saw no other reasonable explanation why a woman her age would suddenly be experiencing such agitation in her chest.

The weird behavior of her heart had nothing to do with the fact that Dr. Zane Bryant was bending over a boy who huddled timidly on the examining table. Absolutely not. After all, she'd spent the last two years since her divorce watching doctors bend over children. There was nothing unusual about the sight.

"That's the best looking doctor I've ever seen," one of the mothers had exclaimed earlier, upon catching sight of Zane. "Are you sure he's a doctor?"

Georgeanne gave a crisp reply. "He's one of the top pediatricians in Houston. We're very lucky to have him."

The woman made a sound—something like "Va-va-voom"—swiveled her hips, and sashayed to a chair with her baby on her hip. Georgeanne smothered her jealousy and laughed with the other mothers. After all, she agreed thoroughly with that assessment.

It had been two weeks since Zane had kissed her in the woods, and not a day went by that Georgeanne didn't relive the experience. Looking at the white cloth of his jacket straining across his shoulders as he pulled up a stool and sat down facing the child on the examining table, Georgeanne longed to slide her hands inside his shirt and jacket and feel the movement of his muscles beneath her palms.

Her mental state deteriorated by the day. As a psychologist, Georgeanne thought she recognized the signs of approaching insanity. If constantly imagining what a man looked and felt like without his clothes wasn't insanity, then what was?

Zane looked up as if he knew she was there. "Come in, please, Georgie. Eric needs someone to make sure I don't get carried away with needles."

Georgeanne knew this meant Eric badly needed someone to hold his hand. No matter how streetwise and cocky a boy might be, a visit to the doctor's office made him feel his mortality. Eric was only nine years old and hadn't been particularly cocky to begin with after stepping on a rusty nail.

"Hello, Eric," she said softly. Zane was paying attention to his patient and didn't notice her embarrassment at being caught loitering in his vicinity. "Dr. Bryant is only joking. He never gets carried away with needles."

Eric watched Zane suspiciously. "He's going to give me a technic shot."

"A tetanus shot? Well, what's one shot among friends?" Georgeanne took Eric's hand. "You know how it is when you go barefoot during the summer. Nails are an occupational hazard."

"Smart woman." Zane filled a syringe as he spoke, and Eric's eyes followed it with fascinated terror. "Eric is one smart fellow himself. He rode his bike out here on his own because he knew he needed treatment. Not many boys his age would have had the sense to do that."

"No, indeed." Georgeanne squeezed Eric's hand gently while Zane swabbed a spot on his skinny arm with alcohol. "Riding five miles on a bicycle with a sore foot is no little accomplishment. We're very proud of you, Eric." She had interviewed the child and knew exactly where Eric lived and how far he had ridden to get to the clinic. "Stop by my office as soon as you're through, and I'll give you a donut and milk. You'll need some energy to get home on."

Eric's thin face lit up at the mention of the donut. Although he kept a close eye on Zane's activities, he hardly jumped when the needle pricked his skin because Georgeanne was directing his attention to the front office, where an appetizing spread of donuts and juice and milk had been set up beside her desk.

"Tell me more about your bike ride, Eric." The glance Zane gave Georgeanne expressed his appreciation of her help. "No wonder you were limping a little when you came in."

Much gratified, Georgeanne listened in admiration while Zane questioned the child. He used a circuitous approach that extracted the necessary information from the most secretive children. Eric, for instance, knew he needed a tetanus shot, but he wasn't about to admit that his foot showed symptoms of infection and needed treatment also.

Within minutes, Zane had the boy's left shoe off. Eric clutched her hand, and Georgeanne obligingly remained beside him in spite of the over-filled waiting room.

"Did you ever have to go to the doctor after stepping on a nail, Georgie?" Zane turned away and readied another syringe.

"I got a huge splinter in the bottom of my foot once when I was eight." Georgeanne admired the sure, deft motions of Zane's big hands. "The main thing I remember about it was that I was terrified Daddy would find out, so I kept quiet for almost a week. He'd have used his pocketknife to dig out the splinter."

That got Eric's attention. "His pocketknife? Gee."

"That's what I thought," Georgeanne agreed. "When I finally had to tell him, Daddy took one look and didn't bother with the knife. He hauled me straight to the emergency room."

"I hope they lectured you for an hour about the folly of letting a splinter remain in your foot for a week," Zane said.

Georgeanne laughed. Eric took comfort in her laughter and barely noticed that Zane was using a needle to deaden the injury before probing the area with a metal instrument.

"I was so relieved to have the operation over with and the splinter out, I didn't mind." She patted Eric's shoulder, and Eric glanced away from Zane's ministrations for a moment. "Fortunately, Eric is smarter than I was. He got here soon enough to be still walking."

Zane looked up, grinning. "And you weren't?" He swiftly cleaned Eric's wound.

"I'm afraid not," Georgeanne squeezed Eric's hand. "I was scared to death."

"You couldn't walk?" Eric asked, interested. "It hurt that bad?"

Georgeanne nodded solemnly. "I kept waiting for it to go away on its own. Instead, it got infected. By the time I had to tell Daddy, it hurt so much, I couldn't touch my foot to the floor."

Zane applied anesthetic. "Shame on you, Georgie. You're a bad example to children everywhere."

"I'm afraid so," Georgeanne said. "The thought of Daddy and his pocketknife effectively sealed my lips."

"I don't blame you." Eric's spirits appeared to lift magically when he saw that Zane had finished and was applying a bandage to his foot.

"I'm going to give you another shot, Eric." Zane bagged some sample packets of antibiotics and handed the bag to the boy. "Then I want you to take one of these pills every morning, and one every evening until they're all gone. Do you think you can remember to do that?"

Now that his ordeal was almost over, Eric's bravado returned. "I can count, can't I? Sure, I can remember." He turned to Georgeanne. "Miss Georgie, can I have another donut if you have any left over? It's for my little sister."

"Certainly, Eric." Georgeanne took his hand and helped him down from the examining table. "Do you think she'd like some orange juice or milk to go with it?"

Eric brightened still further, even though Zane approached with another loaded syringe. He nodded vigorously. "I had to use all our money for the shot," he confided.

Georgeanne and Zane exchanged glances while Eric concentrated on the needle. Georgeanne had written inside Eric's folder that Eric and his little sister lived with their father, who was an alcoholic. When their father remembered they existed, he gave Eric money for food. At the age of nine, Eric was an expert at stretching a dollar.

Georgeanne smiled at Eric. "We'll see what we can do about some donuts. But tetanus shots don't cost the whole twenty dollars, so you'll probably get some money back."

• • •

Zane went through preparations for his next patient on autopilot while surreptitiously watching Georgeanne's graceful exit. Her hand lay protectively on Eric's shoulder, and Zane knew she would see to it that Eric left the clinic with most of his twenty dollars—not to mention his pride—intact.

Georgeanne was priceless. Without her, Zane thought he might have run from the subdued pandemonium of the waiting room. Just glancing out there was enough to exhaust a doctor, but Georgeanne had the patients assessed, interviewed, and sorted. He didn't have to do anything but examine and treat.

Zane went to the examining room door and stood where he could watch Georgeanne. While she had been in the examining room with Eric, four more patients had arrived and stood patiently in line before the receptionist's desk.

Georgeanne didn't become flustered or annoyed. She merely packed four donuts and two cartons of milk in a small sack and handed them to Eric, then she collected his twenty dollars and carefully wrote him out a receipt before handing him back seven dollars in change. Eric's ego probably rose ten notches, judging from his important posture before Georgeanne's desk. He marched out with his bag of pills and his little sister's lunch, very much a man who was capable of going to the doctor on his own besides managing to feed his little sister.

"That man's got the lovesick blues," a woman called.

Too late, Zane noticed a group of mothers staring at him. He ducked back inside. He had no business spending valuable practice time gazing at Georgeanne.

He'd resorted to letting her get to know him by telephone during the past two weeks. It was all he'd been able to manage, thanks to his grueling schedule. Zane figured wryly that he probably ought to be ashamed of himself. Talking to Georgeanne every night about the events of his day had been so soothing, he probably ought to pay her for acting as his therapist.

Watching her today as she took patient information, sorted patients between examining rooms, handed out donuts, and answered the telephone, Zane wondered how much longer he should wait before making his intentions very clear to her.

Georgeanne directed the next patient to the examining room Eric had just vacated and filled out forms on the newly arrived patients, while at the same time keeping her eye on the unruly group of children watching Saturday cartoons on the banged-up television set someone had donated. Zane found that he could keep up with her activities by walking back and forth across the examining room.

At half-past noon, Georgeanne left one of the two examining rooms empty and took a sandwich and a soft drink to Zane, who ate it while a young patient waited in the next room.

"Sorry about the lack of help," she said. "We're still getting started, and none of our lab techs or nurses were available today."

"I understand, Georgie. I offered to let the other two doctors rest, since they've been carrying the load all this time." He drank deeply of the soft drink without taking his eyes off Georgeanne. "Has it been like this every Saturday?"

"Actually, it gets a little worse every passing Saturday." Georgeanne glanced around the room in a proprietary fashion. "More people are finding out about the clinic, people who desperately need its services."

"What's Dr. Baghri's plan for getting more nurses and lab technicians?" Zane asked. "I'm having to rely on my instincts rather than bacterial cultures or blood counts."

Georgeanne turned and cast him a glowing smile. "Dr. Baghri has a plan."

"I might have known." Zane had been around Vijay Baghri long enough to realize the man was full of ideas and impetuosity for carrying them out.

"He's got a plan to lobby the president and Congress to pass laws that will allow retired doctors and nurses and lab techs to work in the clinic without having to carry malpractice insurance," Georgeanne said with enthusiasm. "He says we'd have more doctors and nurses than we need if it weren't for malpractice insurance. So he's come up with an idea."

"I'm not sure I want to hear this," Zane said, grinning.

"Sure, you do. It involves sending Dr. Baghri and a couple of local retired doctors to meet with the President's health care committee."

"Are you planning on going along?"

If she did, he might figure out a way to invite himself along. Zane watched Georgeanne fidget slightly as she became aware of his steady regard. That, more than anything, told him she was unused to being the object of a man's intense attention.

"Not me." Georgeanne shook her head. "I'm not very good at public presentations."

"Why, Georgie? You've done more work than anyone to get the Saturday Children's Clinic going. I have a feeling you'd make a beautiful speech on the subject."

"It's Dr. Baghri's idea." Georgeanne fidgeted with the neat packets of sample medicines stored in a cabinet. "Let him do the public speaking about it."

"He is." Zane set his sandwich and soft drink on a nearby counter top and walked over to stand behind her. The scent of lilies tantalized him. "Are you disturbing all those careful little rows for a reason?"

Georgeanne made a nervous movement and knocked an entire row of cardboard-packed antibiotic samples to the floor. "I was making sure the rows were uniform."

"I see." Zane watched her kneel to pick them up, enjoying his effect on her.

He hadn't kissed Georgeanne in two weeks, and the time had nearly come to end the drought. It was too bad he still had an office full of patients to see, but five o'clock would come soon, then he'd have Georgeanne to himself.

"Zane, you're making me very nervous." She looked up at him, smiling. "I'm never this clumsy."

He laughed. "You're talking to a man who first greeted you from a position flat on the floor, remember?" He took some of the antibiotic samples from her and restacked them in the cabinet. "Do you mind if I ask you a personal question?"

"Ask away, but I've already told you the boring story of my life. What else is there to know?"

Zane studied her face and wondered why he kept feeling that Georgeanne had some deep, dark secret. She had the most honest eyes he had ever looked into. Whatever it was, Zane figured it had to carry the same weight in her mind as her father's pocketknife had during her childhood. Georgeanne didn't let much intimidate her.

He reached down to help her up. "Georgie, why did you marry your ex-husband?"

Georgeanne took his hand and rose slowly. "It's funny you should ask that." She avoided his gaze. "It's a question I've been asking myself a lot the past week or two, and I have yet to come up with a really satisfactory answer."

"Believe it or not," Zane said, "that is a satisfactory answer."

She looked at him as if surprised. "I ought to have loved him with all my heart, but actually, it looks as though I was in love with the idea of marriage and children. It's hard for me to believe that after all my training in psychology, I still made a mistake that glaring."

"Come on, Georgie," he said, grinning. "You don't have to feel guilty for the rest of your life because you made a poor choice the first time out. Besides, I have a feeling there were other pressures involved."

"How did you know?" She moistened her lips, and Zane's gaze focused on her mouth. "Maybe I'd better warn Dr. Baghri that I'm not the only one around here with the second sight."

"I don't have any second sight." His gaze lifted to meet hers. "I simply have a good memory. You said you were a disappointment to the aunt who took you in after your parents died, and I assumed attracting a husband might have been an attempt on your part to please your aunt."

Georgeanne's mouth dropped open. "You do have the second sight. That was exactly the conclusion I finally reached, after much introspection and soul-searching, I might add." She paused, shaking her head. "You have no idea how silly I felt when I finally realized that."

Against his better judgment, Zane rested both his hands on her shoulders. As he'd feared, just touching her made his entire body cry out to feel more of her. Regretfully, he let her go and stepped back.

"You aren't silly, Georgie. You were a confused young girl without guidance." He picked up his sandwich again. "I was a confused young man with a less-than-sensible agenda, in spite of all the guidance I had received." He forced himself to eat a bite of the sandwich, but the taste of pimento cheese did nothing to diminish the longing he felt for the taste of Georgeanne's lips. "My mother even warned me that Roxanne wasn't particularly sympathetic to any of my dreams, but I thought I knew better."

Georgeanne smiled. "What was your agenda?"

Zane chuckled and polished off the sandwich in a couple of bites. "My agenda was to prove I was a sophisticated party animal who had attracted a beautiful, sought-after wife. At the time, I was rather full of myself for having finally received my MD degree." He laughed and added, "I think med schools invented residency to do away with the foolish ideas a lot of young doctors have."

"It's too bad they don't have residencies for BS degrees in psychology," Georgeanne said before she hastened back to the front desk.

Zane watched her go and admired the back view of her shapely figure in the plain, wine-colored knit dress she wore. He wondered if he could possibly see all the patients before five o'clock so he could have a bit of extra time with Georgeanne. Looking out over the crowded waiting room of the Saturday Children's Clinic, he knew the answer was not one he wanted to hear right then.

• • •

Georgeanne took her place behind the receptionist's desk once more and wondered at herself. She had thought she wanted Tony Rollins, even though she had avoided thinking of their future beyond the moment when they exchanged kisses at the altar. It wasn't until far too late that she realized she was not going to suddenly start enjoying sex with him the way her friends claimed they did with their husbands. Obviously, that meant something was wrong with her.

Georgeanne winced. She knew now she had never really cared about Tony, yet she'd suffered greatly over her inability to please him.

But Zane was a different story. Already she cared about Zane far more than she'd ever intended to. If she wasn't careful, she'd lose her heart entirely. What was she going to do if he told her she wasn't woman enough to satisfy him?

The question bombarded her all morning. Georgeanne had no answer for it. In fact, she was guilty of several more trips back to the examining room. No doubt she was on her way to the insane asylum.

The old television set didn't help.

"Furthermore, Fritzi Field continues to remain anonymous," a smooth, unaccented male voice intoned. "Can it be that Fritzi Field is the pseudonym of a well-known author? Or is she a first-time author who wrote the book from the depths of her own experience as some suggest. What do you think, Anne?"

Georgeanne sucked in her breath, lifted her head and stared across the room at the television, where a male anchor faced a female anchor from behind a long curving desk.

"No one knows for certain, John," the female anchor chirruped. "But here with us today is Dr. Meade Murgatroyd, a psychiatrist associated with the New York Institute of Sexual Dysfunction. Dr. Murgatroyd, do you think Fritzi Field is a pseudonym for a well-known author, or is she a housewife whose marriage went kaput?"

Georgeanne breathed easier and bent over some papers on her desk. Given these two choices, she thought Dr. Murgatroyd would steer safely clear of the truth.

"Anne, it's very clear from reading her book that Fritzi Field is a very disgruntled, very hurt person, one who has considerable writing and teaching skills."

Georgeanne hid her face behind her papers. Who liked hearing herself described as disgruntled and hurt? She felt like a child sent off to sulk in a corner.

On the other hand, maybe that was exactly what Fritzi Field was—a hurt, disgruntled child who thought she had found an answer. It was too bad Georgeanne now realized Fritzi Field's answer was no answer at all.

"Dr. Murgatroyd, some critics claim Fritzi Field's writing skills aren't hers at all, but are the result of highly skilled editing. Can you tell us anything about that?"

Georgeanne's head snapped up. She glared at the television.

"Fritzi Field again?" Zane asked.

Georgeanne started and scattered papers. Gathering up the papers gave her time to recollect herself. "I'm afraid she's everywhere these days."

Zane handed her a folder and looked toward the television where Dr. Murgatroyd discussed the probable progression of Fritzi Field's writing career in a way that made Georgeanne long to cast her shoe at the screen.

"That's interesting," Zane said. "Conservative estimates put that book at the top of the bestseller lists for another three months at least."

Georgeanne felt the bottom drop out of her stomach. That meant three more months of daily calls from Alice Anson. Three more months of hearing Fritzi Field being discussed every time she turned on a television set. Three more months of fearing Zane would guess the truth before he became tired of her.

"Naturally," Dr. Murgatroyd went on, "we're all wondering what her next book will be about, and when it will come out. Many of our questions about Fritzi Field will be answered when her second book appears."

They all assumed there would be a second book. Why did everyone insist upon pressuring her for a second book? Georgeanne thought of the two boxes of letters to Fritzi Field at home in her closet and smothered a moan.

She did not consider herself a book author. She wrote magazine articles. She intended to keep on writing magazine articles. They were so much easier and faster to write, and delivered no unexpected repercussions.

"Fritzi Field is an editor's dream just now," the male anchor said. "Her career has taken off like a rocket after this single book, which, as far as anyone knows is her first book. Dr. Murgatroyd, what direction do you think Fritzi Field's career as a writer will take now?"

Georgeanne gulped and forced her fascinated gaze away from the television set. She didn't have a career as a writer. What would everyone say if they found out Fritzi Field's real career was as a secretary-receptionist for a couple of country doctors?

"John, after the incredible success of *Faking It*, Fritzi Field will have a tough time retaining the momentum in her career. In order to top *Faking It*, she will have to—"

Someone switched the television to another channel.

"Darn," Zane said mildly. "Just when I was about to find out what could possibly top *Faking It*."

"Be reasonable, Zane. The only thing that could top *Faking It* is discovering that Fritzi Field is a man." Georgeanne drew a sigh of relief. "Here's the file on Dougie McAllister. He's the little boy who's running a high fever in Examining Room One. Jennifer Bentley is in Examining Room Two with a sore throat."

Zane took the folder and stood looking down at her for a moment. "I don't think Fritzi Field is a man. I also don't think any editor wrote so much as a page of that book."

Georgeanne could feel the blood leaving her head and pooling in the vicinity of her stomach. "Really? I didn't realize you had already read it."

"I haven't finished it yet." Georgeanne noted his interested gaze fixed on her fluctuating complexion. "I've just now gotten to the anatomical information. I'll say this for her—my anatomy professor from med school could learn a few things from that book."

Georgeanne wavered between pride in her accomplishment and horror at the thought of what Zane would say if he knew who had done all that careful anatomical research.

"It's her conclusions I take exception to," Zane added. "She's condemning women to remain in dead marriages with unworthy husbands, as if being married is an end in itself." He smiled at her and turned away. "Tell Dougie I'll be with him as soon as I've finished with Jennifer."

Georgeanne sat staring after him a moment. Why had she had been so determined that her own marriage was worth saving?

She thought about it and came to the conclusion that in her case, she hadn't wanted to admit she was a failure as a wife and as a woman. She'd have done almost anything to avoid making that confession, especially to herself.

She went to the first exam room and told Dougie McAllister and his mother that the doctor would be with them in a few minutes, then poked her head into the other, where Zane was peering down a tiny black child's throat.

"There you are, Georgie," he said, as if he'd been hoping she'd come. "Would you mind helping Mrs. Bentley hold Jennifer?"

Georgeanne entered immediately. Mrs. Bentley looked twice as ill as little Jennifer, and Georgeanne wasted no time in helping the woman lie down on the examining table. In another moment, she felt sure Mrs. Bentley would have passed out.

She held Jennifer while Zane examined Jennifer's mother and put in a call for an ambulance. "She needs to be hospitalized immediately. It looks like some sort of acute infection."

Georgeanne, who had already discovered that trouble had been dogging the Bentley family for some months now, laid a gentle hand on the woman's burning forehead. "Don't worry, Mrs. Bentley. I'll take care of Jennifer myself until we can reach Mr. Bentley."

Mrs. Bentley's eyes fluttered. "God Himself must be here in this place," she whispered. "He sent His angels…" Her voice trailed off, and her eyes closed slowly.

"She's unconscious," Zane said in grim tones. "She must have been sick for some time."

"Dr. Baghri has a clinic for adults in the works." Georgeanne cradled little Jennifer and watched him.

Zane looked up from his examination. "Georgie, you should go to nursing school. It's obvious you know almost as much about nursing as a trained nurse."

"I'm a quick study," Georgeanne said, smiling. "One of these days, I would like to go back to school, but it's hard to find the time." She kept her voice light and cheerful, and Jennifer snuggled trustfully in her arms.

"What are you going to study?" Zane took Mrs. Bentley's pulse and temperature with the expertise of long practice.

"I've always wanted to get my master's degree in clinical psychology." Georgeanne sat down on a stool and held Jennifer on her lap. "Have you finished with Jennifer?"

"Jennifer appears to have a mild case of tonsillitis. A course of antibiotics will straighten her out in no time." He took a blanket out of a lower cabinet and spread it over Mrs. Bentley's unconscious form. "I wish I could say the same for her mother. Are you really going to keep Jennifer?"

Georgeanne nodded. "Mr. Bentley just got a job working on an off-shore oil rig. Once I call him, he should be here by late this afternoon."

Zane straightened and looked down at her. "Mrs. Bentley is right. God did send an angel to this clinic when He sent you."

Chapter 9

Georgeanne approached the apartment building in Pasadena, the suburb of Houston where Zane lived, in considerable mental and physical turmoil. Zane had invited her to spend the day with him, since he was on call and wouldn't be able to go anywhere. He claimed she owed him the visit, since he hadn't even gotten to have dinner with her the day before.

Georgeanne had thought it was probably a good thing Zane had been called back to Houston the moment he finished with his last patient at the Saturday Clinic. But that was before he'd invited her to come to his apartment, and like an idiot, she'd agreed.

Her heart hammered and her palms were damp on the steering wheel, and she hadn't even pulled into the parking lot yet. What was she going to be like when she knocked on his door?

She never got a chance to find out. Zane kept a watch for her red SUV and came out on the landing the moment she turned into a parking space.

"I thought you'd never get here," he called, grinning down at her. He wore a pair of dark slacks with a white polo shirt, and Georgeanne caught her breath at his dark-angel beauty.

He started down the steps, and Georgeanne's heart settled into a more normal, but still rapid, pace. She didn't know how to deal with the shaft of pure feminine desire that shot through the very core of her when she saw Zane.

Georgeanne had never experienced desire like this before, but she knew it immediately for what it was. Her training in psychology told her that the feeling had been magnified by the fact that she and Zane had been kept physically apart for the past two weeks, while their minds and hearts had found common ground. If she wasn't careful, she'd start thinking she was in love with Zane just because his very touch made her tremble.

Georgeanne had chosen a slacks outfit in deep sapphire blue with a multi-colored, short-sleeved silk blouse that gave her a crisp, tailored look. She knew she was going to need all the mental fortification she could get.

"Georgie, you look beautiful." Zane reached the vehicle just as she stepped down from it and took her hand. His arms went around her and he pulled her flush against his body. "Sorry, but this is what waiting does to a man."

He kissed her, not at all shy about letting her feel how he wanted her, and Georgeanne kissed him back. For the moment, all her worries fell away.

She smiled at him. "I'm glad I'm here." It sounded inane, but what else could a woman say when she was being rocked by a desire so intense, it left her gasping for air? "Mr. Bentley called this morning. His wife had a kidney infection. She's much better and will be coming home from the hospital this afternoon."

"I'm glad." Zane tugged at her hand. "Come on up. I usually stay close to home when I'm on call, so I picked up some videos and lots of flavored popcorn." He laughed and added, "I sure hope you like popcorn."

Georgeanne replied, "I love popcorn." She also remembered that when Tony Rollins had said something like this, she immediately started thinking more about the food than she did about what Tony might want to do to her in the realm of lovemaking.

With Zane, her first thoughts were hopeful visions of sharing kisses and more on the sofa in front of the television. He smelled of tangy spice, and his skin was warm and rough to the touch. She could hardly wait to get inside his apartment.

He walked her up the double flight of steps. "You said you liked Roy Rogers, so I rented every old Roy Rogers film I could find."

"I love them all. You'll see why I wanted to grow up to be a cowgirl."

They reached Zane's apartment and he ushered her inside. The moment Georgeanne crossed the threshold, two things struck her mightily. One was the warm feel of Zane's big hand, which had slipped beneath her jacket and rested on the colorful, silk blouse covering her lower back. The other was the copy of *Faking It* resting spine up on the coffee table.

Her breath caught in her throat. Judging from the way the book was spread open, he had already read it three-fourths through.

She ought to tell Zane up front that she was Fritzi Field. She had managed to talk herself out of it so far, but the thought had persisted. He could find out at any moment, and when he did, he'd want nothing further to do with her. She ought to tell him now.

But not right away, her heart had cried. Not before she had a chance to feel all the things she now suspected Zane could make her feel.

Perhaps she was just a coward at heart. The fact was she had written a bestselling book, something very few people could do, and she ought to be proud of that fact.

That came home to her when she finally read a few pieces of Fritzi Field's mail. A few letters excoriated her as a lady-libber with no natural womanliness, but the rest of the letters praised her for bringing into clarity an issue and its solution. Alice Anson had been on target when she'd picked *Faking It* as a book that would touch a national nerve.

So why was *Faking It*'s creator so reluctant to receive the accolades due her?

Georgeanne avoided thinking about that. The major reason in her mind right now was because she didn't want to destroy what she was building with Zane Bryant.

So, was she going to wait and destroy the relationship later, when it would hurt Zane and probably devastate her even more?

Georgeanne decided abruptly that she would tell Zane now. Before things went any further. As she should have done two weeks ago. Zane had a right to complete honesty.

Zane saw her gaze rest upon the book. "Did you deliver your opinion on that book to Denise?"

"As a matter of fact, I did." Georgeanne cleared her throat and kept her face averted, ostensibly to lay her purse down on an end table.

She tried to steady herself by looking around his apartment, but she found little to focus her attention on. Zane's living room was bare of clutter and contained only the pieces of furniture necessary to make it a living room, and even those were of a nondescript, masculine nature. The only personal items present were a stack of Roy Rogers videos and a series of cardboard popcorn containers. And his copy of *Faking It*.

Georgeanne averted her gaze.

"Well?" Zane asked, evidently amused by her obvious intent to avoid the question.

"Well, what?" She searched her brain to delay what she was about to say for a few minutes longer. "Heavens, Zane, I feel as though I'm in a motel room or something. You need some fancy pillows to give this room character. Or maybe a leafy, green plant of some sort."

Zane caught her arms and whirled her to face him, laughing. "All right, Georgie. What is it with you and this book? Every time it's mentioned, you get the weirdest expression on your face."

"Now, Zane, that's the way my face always looks." Georgeanne strove for dignity. Tell him now, her brain shrieked.

"Your nose is going to grow, Georgie," Zane said roughly, and wrapped her in a crushing embrace.

She melted into the kiss immediately, and Zane groaned aloud. Her heart rejoiced. He had been wanting her the way she'd been wanting him.

Zane somehow managed to shut and lock the front door while they indulged in another deep, searching kiss. The moment the door had been duly locked, he swept her up in his arms and carried her toward his bedroom.

Georgeanne couldn't believe it. She was no featherweight, but she rode in Zane Bryant's arms, still kissing him, and she had no doubt what his destination was. To make matters worse, she had no willpower or desire to stop him. The buttery feeling in her knees and the anticipatory pounding of her heart told her she'd get no cooperation from them.

Zane laid her on his queen-sized bed the way he'd place a child on his examination table—with infinite care. He gazed at her intently.

Georgeanne's mouth went dry. Now, just when she needed her powers of speech in order to tell him about Fritzi Field, she couldn't have said a word if she wanted to. So this was what the big deal was...the feeling that every human being craved.

Zane gently removed her shoes and dropped them on the floor beside the bed. Then, with great tenderness, he removed her jacket and tossed it over the head of the bed. He removed his own shoes and came down beside her, stroking his hands over her silk-clad arms.

"Oh, Georgie, you feel so good," he whispered against her cheek, and she felt his long lashes brush her nose. "I've been waiting all week just to touch you again."

Georgeanne's arms went around him, telling him without words that she felt the same. She closed her eyes. At the moment, she was in the serene state of acceptance, knowing what was about to happen and lacking any intent of fighting it.

"I didn't mean to do this," he murmured. "At least, not right off. But I've known for the past two weeks that you were the only woman for me. Georgie, talk to me. Tell me you feel the same."

Georgeanne opened her eyes and found Zane's intense gaze on hers. She had to try twice before she could speak.

"I've known it, too, Zane. I—there's something—"

But Zane had buried his face against her neck with a triumphant laugh. "I knew I couldn't be the only one feeling this way. Oh, Georgie, nothing has ever been like this."

The longer Zane's big hands traveled up and down her sides and her arms, the less interested Georgeanne became in telling him about Fritzi Field. She sucked in air when his hands rested over her breasts, fascinated by the reaction of her own body to his barest touch.

"The doctor is in, Georgie." Zane's deep voice created a further seduction of her senses. "You'll have to take off all your clothes for the examination."

She stared back at him, conscious that the movement of her breasts as she breathed caused his hands to move also. "I will?"

"Yes."

She didn't even have to think about it. "Okay."

"Do you think you can manage it without moving?"

"Sure."

She lay still, and he didn't move either. They basked in their togetherness after the long weeks of separation. Time halted. Even the air seemed golden with promise.

Soon, touching her through her clothes wasn't enough for Zane. He began the task of separating her from her garments, a task usually facilitated by the fact that his patients were so little, he had no trouble skimming a shirt off, or removing a diaper or lowering a pair of trousers. Georgeanne reflected that her clothes must have approximately one-thousand strange fastenings, none of which Zane understood.

Georgeanne didn't help him. She felt far more interested in slipping her hands beneath his shirt to examine his chest with her palms.

"Hey, I'm the doctor here." He looked down at her long, slender hands resting on his bare chest and drew in his breath. "The patient is not supposed to distract the doctor."

"I'm a little worried." Georgeanne's voice was slightly slurred with desire. "You feel as though you could be developing a slight fever."

"Slight fever, nothing," he said roughly. "I'm burning up."

He got her blouse off at last and tossed it over the headboard. Georgeanne wore a lacy brassiere that even Zane's clever fingers could not detect which direction would unlock the hooks. It came loose at last, and rather than remove it, he simply pushed it up to gaze on her with rapt attention.

"You're the most beautiful creature I've ever seen," he said. "I could look at you all day."

Georgeanne's laughter strangled in her throat. "Please don't. I don't think I could stand it."

"Lord, Georgie, nothing has ever been like this. Nothing," he repeated and stroked his palms across her lightly.

Georgeanne moaned as swift stabs of feeling shot through her. If she felt like this just from his barest touch, what was she going to feel like when his lovemaking became serious? Georgeanne moaned again at the very thought of it.

Zane jerked his polo shirt off over his head and tossed it to the floor. "Ordinarily, I don't approve of patients trying to examine the doctor, but this is one time I'll gladly make an exception."

Georgeanne stared at Zane's chest. It was broad with muscle and thickly covered with dark, tightly curling hair. "That's the best looking doctor's chest I've ever seen."

"How many have you seen?"

"Dozens." Georgeanne plowed her fingers through his chest hair, loving the way he threw back his head slightly and sighed with pleasure.

"Oh, yes? Well, you must be one of those doctor-hopping patients. I've got news for you, lady. You've just looked on the last doctor's chest you're ever going to see."

Georgeanne's eyes widened and she gave a small spurt of laughter. "Really? This should be interesting."

"It will be," he said, eyes dark with promise. "I'll probably find it twice as interesting."

He leaned over her, taking her mouth in a hungry, demanding kiss, and Georgeanne arched to kiss him back. The action brought her bare breasts into contact with his chest, creating a thousand pinpricks of desire across her sensitized skin.

Georgeanne had never felt anything like it. Every part of her body seemed to have nerve endings, and every one of those nerve endings screamed for Zane's touch. When they got it, they screamed even louder with pleasure. With all the racket going on, it was a wonder Georgeanne made any sense at all out of the careful examination Dr. Zane Bryant made of her body.

"I've always admired a doctor's hands," she whispered at one point. "They're so tender and experienced. No one can touch a person the way a good doctor can."

"Georgie, for you I'm not just a good doctor." His hot gaze held hers. "I'm a great doctor."

"I'll go along with that." Georgeanne locked her hands behind his head and pulled him down for a lingering kiss.

What surprised Georgeanne the most was the interest she had in examining Zane's body. She had never been particularly interested before in a man's body before, but Zane's was different. Everything about it fascinated her.

She took her time performing a leisurely examination. Every gentle touch of her fingers, every kiss, and every movement of her hands evoked groans or murmurs of delight. Strange, but she'd never realized before how responsive a man could be to a woman's touch. Perhaps it was because she had never been particularly interested in spending time touching a man before. She couldn't get enough.

"If you don't stop," Zane whispered, "there won't be anything left of me."

Georgeanne laughed wickedly and continued with what she was doing. How could she stop, when there was so much enjoyment in it for her?

The world spun. She lay on her back looking up at Zane, whose eyes were dark with passion.

"Georgie, you're about to be on the receiving end of some of that. I hope you've got a lot of stamina."

"Oh, I do," she said. "I do."

"If you keep saying things like that, you're going to need twice as much stamina."

Georgeanne hoped so. She was finding within herself an enormous capacity for passion.

Zane took his time, and Georgeanne's excitement reached new heights. He kissed her breasts, nibbling at the sensitive tips until they were red and taut.

"Zane, you're driving me crazy." Even her voice shook. "Please…"

"Please keep driving you crazy, or please something else?"

"Everything," she said. "All of the above."

His laughter sounded deep and satisfied, and his voice was none too steady either. "Georgie, you're wonderful."

All the same, Zane spent a little more time sending her into a frenzy of need before he slid between her legs and joined his body with hers.

By then, Georgeanne no longer entertained any doubts about her ability to please him. She no longer thought at all. The only thing she could do was feel, and she felt every touch, every kiss, and every caress in her very core, where the sensations soon built to a flashpoint and exploded into a fiery cascade of pleasure that rendered her limp and satisfied in every cell of her body.

She observed, as if from a great distance, Zane's echoing groan of pleasure, and she felt pleased that he had enjoyed their lovemaking.

They lay entwined together and let consciousness return slowly. Georgeanne knew, in every corner of her being, that everything in her life had just altered somehow, but at the moment, she had no great interest in examining the changes.

"What's that weird sound?" Georgeanne lifted her head off the pillow in search of it. Surely it couldn't be her heart, although she wasn't willing to take any bets.

Zane groaned. It wasn't the sort of groan Georgeanne enjoyed hearing, because it sounded more like, "Oh, no," than it did, "More, please."

"It's my pager," he said. "I have to call in."

"Does that mean what I think it means?" Georgeanne couldn't believe it, in spite of what she knew about doctors.

"Probably." He rolled to the edge of the bed.

His pager was attached to the waistband of his trousers, and Zane had to search a moment before he found it and touched the button that revealed the telephone number he was to call.

After a short, grim, conversation, he turned to Georgeanne. "Believe it or not, I have to go. There's been a bad car wreck, with several people badly injured, including two children. I'm sorry, Georgie. I should have known better than to start something when I knew this could happen." He admired her nude body a moment. "However, I can't regret it, in spite of all the plans I had not to jump on you the minute you walked in the door."

Georgeanne sat up and reached for her blouse, conscious of the smile she could not help that spread across her face. "Dare I say I'm glad you did? Just imagine if that page had occurred a mere ten minutes ago."

Zane laughed. "I might not have heard it for the roaring in my ears. Here." He pulled on his shirt and reached for his robe, which lay across the back of a chair. "You don't have to get dressed right away. Put this on and let me remember how you look in it while I'm at the hospital."

Georgeanne understood the grim expression doctors developed when their patients weren't doing well, and she knew Zane's mind was already at the hospital with the two injured children. She obligingly slipped her arms into the blue velour robe and belted it around her waist.

Zane, fully dressed in the time it took Georgeanne to put on his robe, reached for his car keys and took a moment to stare longingly at Georgeanne. "That robe was made for you. Be comfortable, Georgie. And save me some of that popcorn, okay? I don't know what time I'll be home."

He kissed her, one hard, lingering kiss, and then left, half-running down the stairs to his car. Georgeanne stood in the door and watched him drive away then went back inside, feeling lost.

She saw only one thing to do. Georgeanne marched to the refrigerator, which had been well stocked with cold drinks, poured herself a soft drink over ice, then came back to the living room and put a Roy Rogers video on.

Zane's robe was far more comfortable than her outfit, and it smelled of his favorite crisp spicy aftershave. She snuggled into it and curled up on the sofa, where she sampled some of the flavored popcorn while she watched the movie in a desultory fashion. Since she didn't want to provoke comment, she left Fritzi Field's book where it was, merely shoving two popcorn containers in front of it to screen it from her view.

Someone knocked smartly at the door. Georgeanne started and leaped to her feet. She was not about to answer Zane's door dressed in his robe.

"Open up in there."

It was Zane. Thrilled, Georgeanne rushed to the door, looked through the peephole to be sure, and hastened to unlock the door and pull it open. Just as the door swung open, she remembered Zane had gone to the hospital wearing dark trousers and a white polo shirt topped by a blue wind breaker. This man wore khaki trousers and a plaid shirt and carried a leather traveling case.

"Well, well," he said. "What have we here?" He remained on the doorstep, staring at her with deep interest.

Hunter Howell had picked today, of all days, to pay Zane a visit. He was amazingly like Zane, except for certain nuances of expression and the more backswept style of his dark hair. She looked closer and realized that where Zane's expression was open and interested, Hunter Howell's was closed in and wary. The contrast showed all too clearly the differences in their upbringing.

"You must be Zane's brother." She couldn't turn him away, not when he probably didn't see Zane very often. "Please come in. Zane had to go to the hospital. He should be back…sometime soon." She stepped back, checking to see that Zane's robe was securely wrapped.

"Right." Hunter strolled inside with an attitude Georgeanne had often seen in young boys trying to impress the clinic staff with their fearlessness. "I was just passing through on my way to New York, and thought I'd stopover in Houston. But if he already has company, maybe I'd better not stay."

"Only for the day," Georgeanne interrupted hastily. "Please sit down. I hope you like Roy Rogers and flavored popcorn."

Hunter surveyed the cartons and the shoot-out taking place on the television screen. "The popcorn, yes. Roy Rogers is a pleasure I've missed until now." He looked at her, and his gaze suddenly went hard and assessing. "I don't care to interrupt anything. I'd better check back later."

Georgeanne realized two things; one, that Hunter had probably taken a taxi from Houston Intercontinental and had dismissed it, and two, that he fully expected her to make a pass at him. He reminded her so much of a truculent little boy, she couldn't be angry.

"Actually, I'd better be the one to leave," she said. "You probably don't get to visit with him very often, whereas I live nearby. Please make yourself comfortable."

She didn't give him a chance to reply and fled to Zane's bedroom. Fully dressed, she entered the living room and found that Hunter had made himself at home with a beer and the popcorn, and stared in amazement at the movie, although he rose immediately when he saw her.

"This isn't bad," he said, indicating the popcorn. "Did you make it?"

"Zane picked it up at—" she checked one of the cartons "—Imelda's Popcorn Palace. Please tell him that he can call me later tonight."

"Not so fast." Hunter moved with casual grace to block her exit. "You haven't told me your name."

"I'm Georgeanne Hartfield." She sought for something else to add, but there was nothing she could say unless she cared to ask for his autograph. She didn't.

"Hartfield." He scanned her tall figure in a way that made Georgeanne stiffen automatically. "You're the person he's been talking with about opening a clinic for people without insurance, right? Well, well."

Georgeanne said nothing. This was Zane's brother, she told herself. He probably thought he was protecting Zane.

"You are the one, aren't you?" he asked.

"Yes," Georgeanne said. "I'm the one. Excuse me, please. I'd better be leaving."

"What's your hurry? Are you afraid I'm going to attack you?"

"I think you have that backwards, Mr. Howell." Georgeanne's full mouth tightened. "Now get out of my way before I decide you're enough like Zane to be worth attacking."

He burst into delighted laughter. "That's good. That's very good. It put me in my place nicely. Please don't go, Georgeanne." Zane's open charm lit Hunter's gray eyes, temporarily depriving Georgeanne of her breath. He gestured toward the sofa. "My brother will get home and kill me. There's no way he's going to think I'm an adequate substitute for you."

"The two of you have a lot to catch up on, I'm sure." Georgeanne edged toward the door. "He can call me anytime."

"For that matter, he can call me anytime," Hunter said, in his sardonic way. "Come sit down, Georgeanne Hartfield. I'm now convinced that you aren't going to expect me to carry on where Zane left off."

Georgeanne suppressed a smile. "Is that right? What makes you think that?"

"I can tell when a woman isn't interested as well as any other man. Now come sit down before Zane shows up and wants to know what I've done with you."

Georgeanne sat down on an easy chair while Hunter shut off the Roy Rogers movie and settled on the sofa to study her.

"You're not the sort of woman I'd have expected my brother to go for," he said. "On the other hand, what do I know about his tastes?"

There was nothing she could reply to this, so Georgeanne said nothing.

"But you have honest eyes, in addition to your obvious beauty." Hunter looked her over carefully. "I can see why you would appeal to him."

"Thank you, I think." Georgeanne, unembarrassed, looked him over also and smothered surprise that Hunter Howell thought she was beautiful, until she decided he was being polite.

"Yes, I see it now." Hunter narrowed his gray eyes. "You have a lot of strength and compassion. Zane has had it with women who think of nothing but their careers."

Georgeanne gulped. She didn't need to hear what Zane wanted or didn't want in a woman. Not when she still had to tell him about *Faking It*. She'd talk a minute or two more, and then she was leaving—she didn't care what Hunter Howell said.

"Perhaps you should consider writing a book telling women what men want," she said.

"You mean, write one of those horrific pop advice books?" Hunter's beautiful mouth, so like Zane's, twisted in a way that Georgeanne was sure Zane's had never twisted. "Hellish, isn't it, what people read for advice? Take that book." He indicated *Faking It*. "Now a woman is supposed to trick a man into thinking she's enjoying herself when she isn't."

Georgeanne bristled. "Have you read it?"

"I was on a talk show where they discussed it last week." He pinned her with an accusing gray stare. "Why are you reading it?"

Georgeanne could almost hear the lecture trembling on his lips. "It isn't mine. It's Zane's. Now, if you'll excuse me—"

"It's Zane's?" Hunter eyed the book incredulously. "Why on earth is he reading that?"

"You'll have to ask him, Mr. Howell."

A key sounded in the lock, and Hunter turned his head toward the door. "I think I will."

• • •

Zane stepped inside, and his hungry gaze was met, not by Georgeanne still wearing his robe as he'd half-hoped, but by his brother, waving a familiar book at him. Zane forced himself to adjust to the new scenario. "Hi, Hunt. I thought you were in Los Angeles."

"Why the hell are you reading this crazy book?" Hunter demanded. "Are you going to start suggesting it to your patients who are having trouble in their marriages?"

Zane located Georgeanne, who perched uncomfortably on an easy chair near the door. "My patients aren't old enough to be married," he said. "I'm reading it because everywhere I go, people are arguing about it and asking Georgie's opinion on it. I want to see what has everybody so stirred up."

"Oh, yes?" Hunter followed his twin's rapt gaze, then studied Zane's face in a knowing way. "She's an expert on this book?" He grinned suddenly. "How nice for you."

Chapter 10

"Everyone seems to think she's an expert on it," Zane said, his gaze still focused upon Georgeanne. "She's a psychologist."

"Whoa," Hunter said. "Do you mean I've been talking to a psychologist for the past ten minutes?"

Georgeanne's face turned semaphore red, Zane noted, the moment Hunter asked if she was an expert on *Faking It*.

She stood, with a look of determination on her face. "You're quite safe, Mr. Howell. Although I have a degree in psychology, I've never practiced as a psychologist. Zane, I'd better be going. You and your brother probably have a lot to talk about."

"Hold it, Georgie. You aren't going anywhere." Zane came swiftly to her side and slipped one arm around her waist. The other hand he held out to Hunter. "Is there something wrong with your telephone?"

Hunter roared with laughter, flung his arms around his brother and hugged him, then collapsed back onto the sofa. "What he means is, I'm very much in the way," he confided to Georgeanne. "Georgie was too kind-hearted to chase me off, seeing that I've come all this way and my taxi had already driven off, so you're stuck with me," he told Zane. "Besides, you're the oldest. It's your job to look out for me while I'm in this city."

Zane saw that Hunter had instantly assessed his relationship with Georgeanne and had adopted her nickname accordingly. "I'm the oldest by a whole ten minutes." Zane pulled Georgeanne closer. "Georgie, I'm sorry about this. In Hollywood, the stars never dial the phone themselves. If no one is around to do the dialing, their relatives don't get notified of their impending descent."

"I'd have had my agent update my Twitter account if I'd thought of it," Hunter said, grinning. "I'm too fascinated by the fact that Georgie's a psychologist and an expert on this book to leave now. I have it straight from a famous psychiatrist that the author is definitely a man-hater. What do you say, Georgie?"

Zane could almost feel Georgeanne's quandary. She wanted to answer, and she wanted to avoid answering, but why, he could not fathom. Definitely, something about this book called forth a deeply felt response from Georgeanne, not to mention almost every other woman of his acquaintance.

Georgeanne spoke at last. "If she was a man-hater, she'd advise women to get a divorce and stick the men with the bills."

Zane hugged her. "Well said, Georgie."

Georgeanne turned to him. "How are the children, Zane? Did you get there in time?"

"They weren't badly injured, thank God." His face softened as he looked at her. "One had a broken arm I had to set, and the other had a cut that needed stitches. The parents weren't so lucky, I'm afraid. They're both in intensive care."

For a long time, Zane's adoptive parents had been the only people who cared whether or not he helped a child. Looking into the deep brown wells of concern that were Georgeanne's eyes, Zane knew what he'd been missing for the past few years.

He pulled her close and wrapped his arms around her, then rested his cheek against her silky hair, drawing in comfort like air. It felt so good to be with Georgeanne after the tense atmosphere of the hospital emergency room. He closed his eyes and let the stress and the memory of blood, anguish, and injuries drain out of him while he held her and thrilled to the gentle pressure of her hands on his shoulder blades.

Hunter, with the sixth sense he often displayed where Zane was concerned, said nothing. Only the steady crunch of popcorn betrayed his presence. Zane stood and soaked up the feel of Georgeanne's shapely body, the odor of lilies mingled with the odor of popcorn, and the soft sounds made by the brother he hadn't known he had until three years ago. He loved being among people who cared how he felt at times like this.

"That's better," Zane said, at last. "Now I can be human again, until the next call. Georgie, we may as well entertain this bum, since it's obvious he isn't going to go away."

"Not me. The food's too good here." Hunter popped open another carton of flavored popcorn and sampled it. "Let's get back to this book."

"I'm sick of hearing about that book," Zane said. "Let me finish reading it, then I'll favor everyone with a pediatrician's learned opinion of it."

He kept his arm around Georgeanne's waist and guided her to the sofa. He detected her discomfort with the situation but he admitted to himself he did not want to let her leave.

"Come on, Georgie," Hunter coaxed. "You were doing so well. We've settled that the author isn't a man-hater. So what if she's like Zane's ex and would rather think about her career than how to please her man?"

"Let's leave my ex out of this." Zane accepted a handful of cinnamon-flavored popcorn from his brother's box. "She only enjoyed sex with someone capable of advancing her career. Otherwise, she never bothered to fake a thing."

Georgeanne flushed again. Zane started to apologize but thought better of it. Georgeanne deserved to know these things.

"We're embarrassing Georgie," Hunter observed, clearly fascinated.

"I'm not embarrassed. My complexion has a life of its own." Georgeanne sounded resigned. "Zane can tell you that."

"That's definitely true when that book is discussed," Zane said. "That's why I'm reading it. I want to see what it says that sends Georgie's complexion into such fits."

Georgeanne promptly paled.

"So what about it, Georgie?" Hunter said, grinning, his gray gaze narrowed on her. "Do you think women like Zane's ex are reading this book and getting a few pointers?"

"Most women wouldn't be interested in going through all the trouble of tricking men into thinking they were enjoying sex," Georgeanne said. "The women Fritzi Field is advising are women who want to save their marriages, women who feel that their lack of ability to experience sexual pleasure is a major problem in their marriages."

"Everyone is right," Hunter said to Zane. "Georgie is an expert on this book."

"Well, I don't see what all the fuss is about." Zane kept an arm around Georgeanne's stiff shoulders, as she looked ready to claim urgent business elsewhere. "Any man worth his salt would know if his woman was faking her fun."

"What do you say, Georgie?" Hunter asked, as if he'd known her all his life.

"I think that's the whole point," Georgeanne said, after a moment of silence. "The men Fritzi Field is talking about tend to be the sort who probably won't know. They…don't think any of the problem might be with them, and they demand that their wives respond to a technique that isn't working. So Fritzi tells those women to give their husbands what the husbands think they want."

"Serves the husbands right, is that it?" Zane asked.

Georgeanne moved uncomfortably, probably disconcerted by the twin gray gazes fixed on her face, Zane decided. If he had any sense, he would change the subject. Georgeanne looked close to bolting for the door.

"That was more or less my impression," she hedged.

"Georgie, you're pretty good at this," Hunter said, in admiration. "How would you like me to mention you to a couple of talk show hosts? I'm on my way to New York for some publicity shows."

Georgeanne looked absolutely horrified. "Thank you, but no. I wouldn't go on a talk show if I'd written the book."

"Ah-ha," Hunter said, in the teasing tones of a little boy. "The psychologist needs psychoanalysis. She's scared."

"Leave her alone, Hunt." Zane saw the irrepressible fun in his brother's gray eyes and felt the incredible tension in Georgeanne's lithe body where it was pressed against his.

"He's right," Georgeanne said. "Appearing on a talk show would probably give me a heart attack."

Zane wondered why the thought of it unnerved her so much, since Georgeanne was unlikely to go on any talk shows, no matter how brilliant her analysis of *Faking It*.

"Be a sport, Georgie. I could give your name to a few of the talk show hosts I happen to know," Hunter said, grinning wickedly. "You can be a resource person. You know more about that dumb book than anyone else I've heard. You'd be a hit."

"If anyone calls me, I'll say I've never even heard of the book, much less read it," Georgeanne said.

"Cease and desist, Hunt," Zane said. Georgeanne's fingernails were actually digging holes in the soft skin of her own hands. "You're upsetting her."

Hunter stared at Georgeanne's tense, pale face. "By God, I have. Sorry, Georgie. I mean, I know talk shows are definitely low-class entertainment, but they're nothing to be scared of."

"I'm not upset," Georgeanne stated, in the tones of one seeking to convince herself.

"I thought psychologists loved advising people," Hunter said. "Just think of being able to advise thousands of people at one time."

Georgeanne forced a smile, although Zane would have sworn the thought affected her much like being zapped with a Taser. "I've never practiced as a psychologist."

"I thought psychologists automatically analyzed everyone," Hunter said. "Do they ever psychoanalyze themselves?"

Zane decided Hunter's teasing had gone far enough. Then he noted that, for some reason, this question acted upon Georgeanne like a tranquilizer.

She smiled. "I read once that people majored in psychology in order to figure out what was wrong with themselves. Maybe it's true."

Zane caught the gleam of fun in her deep brown eyes and closed his mouth again. He should have known Georgeanne wouldn't let Hunter's teasing get to her.

"So what have you found out?" Hunter stared at Georgeanne's face in obvious fascination.

"After deep analysis, I discovered that what I'd guessed all along was true," she announced, in solemn tones. "I was so used to standing out when I didn't want to simply because of being so much taller than everyone else that I became very sensitive about it. Public speaking is a traumatic experience for me."

"You need therapy," Hunter decided. "An intensive session on the 'Tonight Show with Jay Leno' would set you straight instantly."

"There is no way that I will appear on any talk show and talk about any subject," Georgeanne said. "For one thing, I am not an expert. For another, there are plenty of people out there who are. Let them do it."

"But you make the most sense of anyone I've heard when it comes to *Faking It*," Hunter argued. "You owe it to the American reading public."

"Why is it people always drag in patriotism when they want someone to do something?" Georgeanne asked Zane.

"I don't know, but I'm sure a psychiatrist would have a field day with him," Zane said. "Got any friends who wouldn't mind a Hollywood prima donna on their couches?"

"No one wants to hear what I think about *Faking It*," Hunter said, "but they'll eat Georgie up. She made better sense in ten minutes than those psychiatrists did in a whole half-hour of arguing."

"That's because she's well-trained enough to read the book before she tries to talk about it," Zane said. "Right, Georgie?"

"That probably has a lot to do with it," Georgeanne agreed, relaxing a little.

Hunter found that exquisitely humorous. "If you ask me, that probably has everything to do with it."

• • •

Georgeanne did not know what would be worse, going on a talk show as Fritzi Field or spending the rest of the evening in Zane's living room with Hunter Howell quizzing her about *Faking It*. She began searching for reasons to hasten home immediately.

She had no idea how long Hunter would remain and she didn't like to ask. She hadn't even had a chance to think on what she had shared with Zane in the bedroom earlier, and something told her the experience had changed her in ways she needed to consider.

"Forget it, Georgie," Zane said, narrow-eyed. "You are not leaving."

"Why does she want to leave?" Hunter asked. "Is my face putting you off, Georgie? I can put on my dark glasses if you think that'll help."

Georgeanne wondered why everybody in the world could read her thoughts. "I'm not leaving." She seized a carton of flavored popcorn and dug in. "But I am getting hungry."

Hunter jumped up and headed for the kitchen. "She needs coffee. I'll go make some. What about a frozen dinner? He's got loads of them in his freezer. I'll fix one for you."

Georgeanne stared after him, and then looked at Zane. "What on earth was that all about?"

"I think he's decided I need a few minutes alone with you to talk you out of leaving. I told you Hunt has a sixth sense." Zane tilted her chin up with one big hand and cupped the other around her shoulder. "Sorry about his showing up like this. He isn't used to finding a woman in my apartment."

Georgeanne laughed. "So I gathered. I enjoyed talking to him." She added, smiling, "By the way, everything I said in my analysis of him still goes. He's very concerned about your happiness, which is why he decided he'd better check me out thoroughly."

"Remind me to kill him," Zane said. "This isn't the weekend I had planned for us, Georgie. For one thing, I didn't intend to fall into bed with you right off. For another, I didn't plan to introduce you to Hunt until after we were well established as a couple."

"You'd have run into a problem there." She smiled at him, well aware that memories of their lovemaking probably showed on her face. "Your brother is very protective of you."

"I'll definitely have to kill him." He brushed his lips over hers. "The thing is, I didn't want our first time together to be a quickie, and that's what it's turning out to be."

"It still ranks as the most memorable experience of my life." Georgeanne felt the telltale heat radiating from her face when the meaning of her own words registered in her head. "We knew you were on call, so please don't blame yourself."

"Georgie, that is without a doubt the best thing a woman has ever said to me." Zane kissed her in earnest. "I'll have to find some way to reward you."

So much for hoping Zane had not picked up on her statement. "I'll look forward to that reward."

"Mexican or turkey?" Hunter called from the kitchen.

"Mexican," Georgeanne answered, without hesitation.

"I think I like being the one to show you everything you missed during your marriage," Zane said.

Georgeanne flushed and looked away. "Is it so obvious? I thought I was more mysterious than that."

Zane laughed. "Confess, Georgie. You were hoping for a one-night stand."

"A what?" Georgeanne's mouth dropped open. "Me?"

Zane chuckled. "I'm only teasing. If there's one thing a biology major such as myself usually runs from, it's casual sex. And sex with you is anything but casual. That's why I want to be sure you understand that this is a relationship, and there's nobody but you in my life."

Georgeanne stared into his determined gaze in wonderment. All the books said men were a lot more casual about sex than women, and that women tended to place too much importance on going to bed with a man.

On the other hand, what did she know? The more books Fritzi Field sold, the more ignorant Georgeanne considered herself about sex, marriage, and everything else that had to do with men.

"Why do biology majors such as yourself run from casual sex?" she asked.

"Have you any idea how many hours I spent peering at germs through powerful microscopes?"

"Oh." Georgeanne smiled and wished she had known Zane in his student days. "Maybe microbiology should be a requirement for high school students. It might turn out to be the best sex education tool in existence."

"Speaking of sex education," Hunter said from the kitchen door, "I'm contacting my agent tonight. I've got to play the lead role when *Faking It* is made into a movie."

Georgeanne felt the blood leaving her face as the bottom fell out of her stomach.

"It's my new career goal," Hunter added. "I've got to play the man who convinces the author of *Faking It* that she no longer needs to fake it."

Georgeanne promptly turned the color of ripe tomatoes and wished for a tornado that would pluck her bodily out of Zane's living room. She made a sound somewhere between those made by deflating balloons and dying ducks.

"There she goes again, Zane," Hunter said, deeply interested. "I didn't know women could still blush like that."

Georgeanne grabbed for her slipping dignity with all her might. "I'm probably the only one left. That's a very peculiar career goal, Hunter. I thought you made your living being a macho career soldier with a tender but carefully hidden heart."

"I've ditched the action-adventure stuff. I'm now into playing neurotic New Yorkers."

"Is that the sort of man you figure will convince Fritzi Field that love is never having to fake it again?" Zane asked.

"I wish you'd stop laughing like that," Hunter complained. "You're going to ruin my new career goal."

"Sorry." Zane looked at Georgeanne, still chuckling. "If he starts playing neurotic New Yorkers, I'm quitting the movies."

Georgeanne said nothing and ate a handful of cinnamon-flavored popcorn. Under the circumstances, she considered it the only viable option.

"On the other hand, maybe I'll get a part in one of those television doctor-and-hospital dramas." Hunter remained in the kitchen door, leaning against the doorframe. "That would give me plenty of opportunity to address this book."

"Now that you're making a lot of money in the movie business, maybe you can write your own book," Zane said. "You could take a year off and hire a ghost writer. What about it, Georgie? You'd probably do a great job as Hunt's ghost writer."

Georgeanne thought about it for precisely one-one-hundredth of a second. "I'm not a writer. I'm a secretary-receptionist at a medical clinic."

"Whether you know it or not, you're a writer," Zane informed her. "You write magazine articles, don't you? And you write killer sales letters about the Saturday Children's Clinic."

She caught her breath, all too conscious of Hunter's interested stare.

"She really writes magazine articles?" Hunter asked.

"I'm in the process of getting a collection of them," Zane said. "She had one in this month's *Women's Journal.*"

"That's fantastic, Georgie." Hunter grew more enthusiastic by the minute. "It's time to change our lives for the better and become famous authors. I'll dictate and you can put everything I say about *Faking It* into more erudite terms. What do you say?"

Georgeanne wondered what kind of prison term she would get if she shoved Zane's copy of *Faking It* down Hunter Howell's throat. "I say, where's my Mexican dinner? A person could starve to death thinking about all that work."

Hunter laughed and vanished back into the kitchen.

"Sorry about Hunt's sense of humor." Zane draped his arm around her shoulders and leaned back, pulling her with him.

"You should encourage him to take college classes," she said. "He can always attend an online college."

"True. I'll mention it to him." Zane brushed his lips over her cheek. "What about you, Georgie? Are you still cherishing dreams of going back to school?"

Georgeanne allowed herself to sink back into Zane's embrace. "I thought I'd like to practice clinical psychology, but that was before I—" She broke off and felt the telltale heat flood her cheeks.

"Before you what?" Zane asked.

"That was before I realized what a heavy burden giving people advice would be."

If she had realized the weight of that burden before sending *Faking It* off to a publisher, would she have sent it?

Georgeanne honestly could not answer that question.

Chapter 11

Georgeanne ate the Mexican dinner Hunter served up and reflected that she had been so busy dodging repercussions from her unexpected success as Fritzi Field, it hadn't occurred to her that she now had the money to get the extra training she needed in order to practice as a clinical psychologist. She could afford to stop working and go to graduate school.

The idea sounded...depressing. Naturally, the depression registered in full glory on her face.

"Georgie, are you all right?" Zane asked.

"I'm fine," Georgeanne said. "I was just thinking about graduate school."

She didn't want to go back to school. Georgeanne exercised great control to keep from gasping at the enormity of this blasphemy.

"When are you going to have time?" Zane asked. "You work hard enough already."

"I have a lot of energy," Georgeanne said absently.

If she didn't want to go to graduate school, which had been the biggest immediate goal she nurtured, then just what did she want to do?

"I like that," Hunter said. "She has a lot of energy."

"She doesn't know it yet, but she's going to start conserving her energy," Zane said.

Hunter laughed. "Enjoy yourself, brother. Something tells me you're fighting an uphill battle. Say, Georgie, why don't you consider medical school?"

"Maybe *you* should consider medical school," Georgeanne returned, smiling at him.

"She makes it sound so easy," Hunter said, to Zane.

Georgeanne cautiously examined her future, while Zane and Hunter discussed medical school. She hadn't thought about it before, but she now had the money to quit her job and do whatever she wanted to do.

Oddly enough, the only interesting thing that occurred to her was to buy a yellow bikini and a convertible. Picturing herself with both, Georgeanne had to smother laughter.

Her life had once been reasonably simple. She worked at her clinic job while she railroaded Dr. Baghri's idea to completion and wrote about whatever interested her. Why had her long-time dream of graduate school evaporated now that she finally had the money to go?

"Georgie, you're a thousand miles away," Zane said.

"I know." She looked up and smiled at him. "I've just realized I don't want to go to graduate school. After all this time spent wishing I could go, it's something of a shock to realize I've changed my mind."

He laughed and hugged her against him. "You'd be wasted as a psychologist. Your talents are so much broader and more valuable."

Georgeanne turned sparkling dark-brown eyes on him. "I'm glad you think so, because I'm now thinking about leaving the Gant Clinic and applying for a position in your front office."

Zane whistled. "If you worked for me, I can assure you I'd get very little work done."

Hunter laughed. "Very good, Georgie. You've now reduced him to a pile of ashes. Maybe you'd better consider another clinic."

Zane frowned. "She's not allowed to work for any single male doctors, or any male doctor under the age of fifty, or any male—"

"We get the picture," Hunter interrupted. "Okay, Georgie, so now that you've decided graduate school isn't for you, what is it you'd really, really like to do?"

Zane looked at her. "I like her the way she is now, busy with her community projects and her job."

Georgeanne stared at Zane, so like his twin brother, but so uniquely hers. Hunter didn't make her feel as if a thousand candles were lit beneath her skin, or cause her breath to catch in her throat when she looked at him.

"Years ago, I wanted to be a pop psychologist like Joyce Brothers and write books telling people how to live happy lives," she said, before she realized how much the statement revealed.

"Like Fritzi Field?" Zane asked, casting her a grin.

Georgeanne hoped no one noticed the inevitable whitening of her complexion. "Something like that. It was my dream to write a bestselling book on some new theory of love and life."

Writing *Faking It* had been the most challenging, most difficult project she'd ever undertaken, and her every emotion got involved. She'd emerged from the task limp and drained, but with a paradoxically reinvigorated spirit.

"Of course, that was before I—" She choked and coughed while she altered her sentence. "Before I realized that I first needed something valuable to say."

About the time she recovered from *Faking It* and began contemplating a new writing project, bestseller-dom struck. Suddenly, she felt as if she stood in a crowd on the street while all her clothes disintegrated off her body.

"Come on, Georgie," Zane said. "What is it you were really about to say?"

Georgeanne thought fast. "I was going to say, that was before I realized how prideful the whole idea was that I could give people advice."

"You're the least proud person I know." Zane regarded her in silence a moment. "You've sold almost twenty magazine articles. I've got a librarian hunting them for me." Before Georgeanne could recover from the surprise of this, he asked, "Have you ever thought about writing a book?"

"As a matter of fact, I have." She sucked in her breath. Now she'd done it.

"What about?"

Inspiration failed her. She couldn't think of a single thing to say that wouldn't sound silly.

Hunter chimed in. "I still think we ought to do a book that proves Fritzi Field is a quack. What do you say, Georgie? You provide the expertise and I'll do the talk shows. We'll be a bigger hit than Fritzi. You can bank on it."

• • •

Zane noted that Georgeanne's complexion fluctuated so rapidly, if he saw it in one of his young patients, he'd likely call in a vascular specialist for a consult.

"First, you'd have to supply me with all the good reasons why Fritzi is a quack," she said, with admirable composure, considering the way she went from absolutely white to fire-truck red within two seconds. "And there had better be enough of them for me to expound on and fill a whole book."

"We have a physician right here in our midst." Hunter indicated Zane. "He'll provide the scientific reasons, I'll provide the general commentary, and you'll provide all the real work." He appealed to Zane. "Doesn't that sound like a fair split of responsibilities to you?"

"I think our main writer just went on strike for a bigger share of the profits." Zane noted that Georgeanne's hand lay in a relaxed-looking position on the sofa arm, but in reality her fingers clutched the fabric in a death grip. "Let's put on a movie so poor Georgie can relax. All this talk about Fritzi Field is getting to her."

"But it's so fascinating," Hunter protested. "I'm supposed to spend the next two weeks hitting all the New York talk shows to publicize *Breaking Even*, and it doesn't take a nuclear scientist to see that nobody is going to be interested in *Breaking Even* when they can host fights about *Faking It*."

Zane noted that Georgeanne turned perfectly white, then flushed deep red even as she said, "In that case, maybe you'd better skim the book and formulate your own learned opinion on it so you can still dominate the talk shows."

Hunter grinned. "Why don't you save me the trouble by formulating a good opinion for me? My own opinion would probably be uneducated and Neanderthal in nature."

If possible, Georgeanne reddened even more. "In that case, you'd better stick to *Breaking Even*. Otherwise, you'd have to read the book and see what the author is trying to say."

"And just what is it you think the author trying to say?" Zane asked, genuinely curious.

Interestingly, Georgeanne whitened. "The author is telling a specific, small group of women one way they can save their marriages." She hesitated, flushed with fiery color, and added in a barely audible voice, "I'll bet she never expected the book to become a bestseller, or that other people besides those the book was written for would read it."

Zane realized several things in that instant. One was that Georgeanne had nailed the author's intent with deadeye accuracy. And he also knew that Georgeanne spoke for the author when she said she never expected the book to sell millions of copies to people outside the book's core audience.

Zane studied at her profile in wondering silence. Georgeanne Hartfield—the mysterious and reclusive Fritzi Field? That would certainly explain her complexion's behavior every time the book was mentioned.

Suddenly, a vision arose in Zane's mind of two large cardboard boxes sitting on Georgeanne's living room floor that bore the logo of the publisher of *Faking It*.

"You sound like you know Fritzi Field," Hunter said in accusing tones. "Come on, Georgie. Confess."

Zane turned his head to look at his brother. Hunter had also picked up on Georgeanne's uncanny knowledge of the author's mind.

"Not me." Georgeanne gave Hunter a firm smile and shook her head. "If she wants to stay out of the public eye, I'd be the last person to rat her out, even if I knew her identity."

"If you ask me, you do know her identity." Hunter leaned forward, staring at her. "What do you think, brother? Got any truth serum in that black bag of yours?"

"I don't need truth serum to check out Georgie's veracity." Zane couldn't help but grin. "All I have to do is monitor the state of her complexion."

"In that case," Georgeanne said, with enormous dignity, "you may as well shoot me now. My complexion condemns me of any and all accusations at any and all times."

"I have a feeling that wasn't always true," Zane said in his gentlest voice. "Only in the past few weeks, maybe, since *Faking It* hit the bestseller lists."

Sure enough, Georgeanne's face went dead white, then red, and she cast a single startled glance at him before focusing once more on the boxes of flavored popcorn on his coffee table. She said nothing, but Zane saw the white-knuckled grip she acquired on her own hands.

For once, Hunter remained silent. Zane looked across the room at his brother and noted the look of comprehension his twin wore.

Georgeanne regarded the coffee table in the manner of one examining a true work of art.

"Well," Hunter said, breaking the long silence. "This is probably my cue to exit, but without a script, I don't know quite how to go about it."

"You say you're getting really, really sleepy and you could sure use a good nap," Zane said, suppressing a grin.

"Okay." Hunter brightened, and Zane realized his brother knew he needed to be alone with Georgeanne, but did not want to leave the apartment. "I'm getting really sleepy. Mind if I sack out on your bed?"

"Feel free. The bedroom's all yours." Zane draped his arm around Georgeanne's shoulders. "Just make a lot of noise before you come out."

"Will do." Hunter rose with alacrity. "Georgie, I still say you'd be a natural on the talk show circuit. Or maybe you should think about radio interviews if television scares you."

Georgeanne looked up at him, flushing once more. "I'd rather not think about any interviews, thank you."

Hunter threw her a kiss and headed for the bedroom. "I'd kiss you if I wasn't afraid my brother would knock me into the middle of next week. Don't feel you have to go rushing off because of me."

Georgeanne looked after him. "What was that all about? He doesn't look at all sleepy to me."

"He knows I want to talk to you in private, and he also doesn't want to miss the next episode, so he's temporarily adjourning to the bedroom."

"The next episode?" Georgeanne looked at the blank television screen in puzzlement. "Did I miss something?" She met Zane's gaze briefly, then looked away, reddening. "You know, don't you?"

"That you wrote *Faking It*? Yes, and I probably should have realized it a lot sooner, like when I saw those two boxes from your publisher." He drew her closer. "Giving intimate advice on a national scale must have scared you half to death."

"It did." Georgeanne closed her eyes and drew in a deep breath. "All of a sudden, people were literally taking the book to heart. And it was all—" She broke off on a gasp, then repeated, "It was all just theory. That's why I let it go to press. I thought that maybe some other woman out there would read it in time to save her marriage." She added, "If she wanted to, that is."

Zane touched her chin to make her look at him. "Did you want to save your marriage, Georgie?"

She changed color, in true Georgeanne fashion. "At first, I thought I did. It wasn't until I had finished the book and sent it to an agent that I realized…that I realized…" She trailed off, looking horrified.

"Go on, please," Zane said.

She glanced at him, then looked away, flushing again. "I suddenly realized that I was glad he was gone, and that I was no actress. All that acting all of the time would have been wearing, and for what? We would still have fought over the time I spent at the Humane Society, or at the Saturday Clinic." She covered her face with her hands. "I'm a terrible person, telling everybody to do something I couldn't have done myself."

Zane gently pried her hands away from her face and held them in his, noting automatically how cold they felt. "That's because you're basically too honest to pretend for long. The truth is, I don't think you loved him. Not the way you'd have needed to love him in order to pull off a long-term act of the sort *Faking It* advocates."

"I didn't realize that when I wrote the book." She kept her head bent, staring at his hands holding hers. "My pride had been crushed. I felt like a failure, and that everything wrong between us was my fault, so I began writing the book as an analysis of what I thought went wrong and what I could have done about it." She swallowed. "Somehow, after I finished the writing and sold the book, I realized I was actually glad the marriage was over." She added in doleful tones, "Then the book took off."

"What happens now, Georgie?" Zane asked gently. "You appear to have a huge audience waiting to hear from you. What do you intend to do about it?"

"Do about it?" Her huge, brown eyes met his in a startled flash. "Keep dodging my agent's calls, I suppose, and praying that no one figures out who Fritzi Field really is."

"Do you really think that's going to be possible?" Zane still had trouble getting his mind around the idea that Georgeanne Hartfield had a nationwide audience breathlessly awaiting her least pronouncement. "You heard Hunt. The talk shows can't seem to discuss anything else."

"They'll just have to find something." On that, Georgeanne sounded determined. "I have nothing more to add on the subject."

Zane touched his fingertip to her lips and wished Hunter was back in Los Angeles, even though he knew that now was not the time to make love to Georgeanne again, no matter how much he might want to. "In that case, kiss me again and let's talk about this."

Georgeanne stiffened in his embrace. "If you kiss me, I won't be able to talk about anything, much less Fritzi Field."

"I think you'll manage." He smiled into her eyes and kissed her gently. "Georgie, you do realize, don't you, that you're going to have to do something about this?"

"This?" Georgeanne looked dazed, much to his delight. "What do you mean?"

"You're going to have to deal with the Fritzi Field thing, or it's going to blow up in your face. You need to go public at a time you choose. Otherwise, you won't have that choice."

She turned her face away. "Can we please not talk about Fritzi Field? She's trying to take over my life, and that was not what I bargained for when I wrote that book."

"But you have an audience waiting, Georgie. Don't you think they deserve to hear from the author?"

Georgeanne winced. "Are you talking about all that mail waiting at home? I can't possibly read all those letters, Zane. I'd have to quit my job."

She looked so upset, Zane longed to comfort her in the time-honored male way. But sex wasn't what she needed just now. As he saw it, Georgeanne had a real problem, one that was not going to go away unless she dealt with it.

For a moment he considered ignoring the problem right along with Georgeanne, but he fought off the temptation. Whether Georgeanne knew it or not, Fritzi Field could not succeed in remaining anonymous forever.

"The way I see it is this," he said. "Like it or not, you have a responsibility to your readers, and they aren't going to let you remain anonymous for long. One of your fans will succeed in tracking you down, if a reporter doesn't manage it first." He paused and stared into her eyes in all seriousness. "Georgie, you need to come up with a plan."

• • •

Georgeanne drove home in a dither, scarcely able to think. Zane knew she was Fritzi Field. Soon, everyone else in the entire world would, also.

A plan. Zane thought she needed to come up with a plan.

"How about hiding under my front porch?" she had asked. "Isn't that a plan?"

"The sooner you go public, the sooner the fuss will die down," Zane said.

Then Hunter appeared in the bedroom doorway with her purse in his hands. "Your phone is ringing. It might be important."

It was Alice Anson, Georgeanne's agent. What Alice had to say almost jerked the floor from beneath her feet, with the result that Zane and Hunter both wound up soothing her with bowls of flavored popcorn and glasses of wine.

"You've been outed, kid," Alice said. "I don't know who dug it out, but I've been getting calls for the past half hour, and your name and location are popping up all over the Internet. So be warned. Now, about these talk show invitations…"

Georgeanne had managed to end the call without committing herself, only to find Zane and his brother ready to offer good advice. According to them, by tomorrow morning she would probably be headline news in all the local newspapers, and her home phone was probably ringing off the hook with calls from reporters.

She finally left Zane's apartment at two in the morning, sent on her way with several cups of stout coffee—as if she needed coffee to keep her awake after this news.

Then she remembered she had to be at work by eight, and she needed at least a little rest, even though she didn't feel sleepy in the least.

Who was she kidding? She'd disrupt the clinic if she went to work as usual.

She turned in at her own driveway and saw two canine forms arise and stand waiting, along with one human form that reposed on her front porch swing. When she stopped her car before the front steps, she noticed Nurse Denise Devereaux's snappy little red car parked well to the side.

Denise rose in her dignified way and waited while Georgeanne greeted Roscoe and Jack. "Is Fritzi going to get after me for starting a website about her book?" she asked, when Georgeanne straightened.

"She's more likely to offer you a fat fee and ask you to call it the Fritzi Field official website," Georgeanne said in dry tones. "Come on in, Denise."

"At first, my feelings were hurt because you didn't tell me, even after you saw how much the book meant to me." Denise entered and followed Georgeanne into the kitchen. "Then I realized you must have been caught totally by surprise when the book took off like a rocket."

"That's an understatement." Georgeanne, moving on autopilot, put more coffee on to perk and located a fresh box of lemon snap cookies in her cabinets. "I'm still in shock."

"So what are you going to do now, Georgie?" Denise sat down and looked across the table at her friend. "I can understand why you're sort of between a rock and a hard place, what with meeting that stunning Dr. Bryant. I'll bet you're not even interested in your ex-husband anymore."

"You're right about that," Georgeanne dryly. "But Zane thinks I need to do a publicity tour, because the book has such a wide audience now."

"You told him you wrote *Faking It*?" Denise asked, surprised. "Well, he's right. The readers need to hear from Fritzi herself."

"I literally have nothing else to say on the subject." Georgeanne looked into Denise's face in a searching way. "However, it looks to me as though you have a lot to add to what Fritzi had to say."

Denise smiled and took out her smart phone, tapped on the screen a few times, then handed the phone across the table to Georgeanne. "I got my website online last night, and I've already gotten several thousand hits. This thing is big, Georgie. An author almost has to have a website nowadays."

Georgeanne stared at Denise's intense face, then down at the little screen. "Everyone except Fritzi, apparently."

"Fritzi's online now, whether she knows it or not." Denise looked intensely satisfied. "I've posted several essays about some ideas in the book and started a question-and-answer section." Her dark face glowed with excitement. "The questions are pouring in. I can't wait to start answering them."

Georgeanne regarded her friend in disbelief. "You're going to answer questions online from readers of *Faking It*?"

Denise grinned. "Why not? I feel almost like I wrote this book, and since Fritzi isn't talking, I'm going to talk for her. I'm telling you, Georgie, there's a huge need out there, and somebody has to fill it. I'm going to do my best." She added craftily, "And if Fritzi doesn't like what I say, then she'll just have to go public and refute me."

Georgeanne sat for a moment in awed silence, while her brain sifted through the new set of facts. She stared at the tiny screen and absorbed the fact that Denise's Q & A Forum had almost a hundred questions awaiting answers. Then she looked toward her bedroom, where two boxes filled with letters to Fritzi Field took up entirely too much space in her closet.

"Denise," she said slowly, "I think it's time our friendship progressed to a higher level of trust and mutual support. Let's call my agent and discuss this over coffee and cookies."

• • •

A month later, Zane sprawled on his sofa and glared at the television screen, where a talk show host hugged a tall, shapely woman far too enthusiastically. Zane was tempted to fly to Los Angeles and flatten at least five male talk show hosts he could name. They had no business hugging Georgeanne Hartfield. She belonged to him.

In his dreams. Zane leaned back, muttering curses, as Georgeanne seated herself across from the host and smiled graciously. This time, Georgeanne had brought a companion. Denise Devereaux, stunning in a slinky red outfit, also took a hug from the host and sat down beside Georgeanne.

Zane sat up, certain something earthshaking was forthcoming. It had been weeks since Georgeanne took his advice and left her job and her home to do a book publicity tour. He had recorded every single show he could when he was unable to watch her, but Georgeanne onscreen just wasn't the same as Georgeanne in person, preferably in his arms.

He refused to think about the fact that she hadn't called him but one time in the past month. Book publicity tours were whirlwind affairs, or so he understood. She probably didn't have time for conversations with him.

A loud pounding sounded at his apartment door. Zane ignored it on the grounds that it was Friday night.

"I know you're in there," Hunter Howell called. "Open up."

Zane sprang to his feet and flung open the door. Hunt probably knew all these wolfish talk show hosts.

"I know 'em all," Hunter said, when asked. "Just tell me the name, and I'll tell you whether or not to worry. Now move aside and let me in."

Zane scowled. "I thought you lived in Los Angeles."

"Glad to see you, too." Hunter stepped inside and shut the door behind him.

Zane sat down and glared toward the television, where a close-up shot of Georgeanne's face gave him a wrenching pang of loss. "Glendale Guzman is hugging up to her. I'd like to…"

"You should." Hunter came and sat beside him in the semi-darkness. "Old Glen is known for trying to bed his guests."

"What?"

"Just kidding. Relax, Zane. The guy is a happily married man with three little kids. Hugging is his only interviewing skill."

The brothers listened in silence as Georgeanne talked about what it was like to be Fritzi Field and answered questions about *Faking It*. Her replies sounded natural and polished, and Zane sighed. He was so far gone, even her voice over the television set moved him.

"How much longer are you going to put up with this?" Hunter asked, during the first commercial break.

Zane scowled. "With a career like Fritzi Field's, what woman wants to be a pediatrician's wife?" He laughed with some bitterness. "Did I ever tell you that Roxanne was after me to switch to cardiology?"

"Gawd," Hunter said.

"Lots of social prestige in cardiology these days," Zane said. "Don't see anything in it, myself. If people would quit smoking and drinking and get some exercise..."

"Georgie seems to like pediatricians. Who's that with her?"

Zane scowled again when the talk show resumed. "It's one of the nurses from the clinic where Georgie works. She's big fan of Georgie's book."

Georgeanne said in her rich voice, "Glen, I'd like to introduce you and the viewers to Fritzi Field's official spokeswoman, Ms. Denise Devereaux. She's the administrator of 'Fritzi's Front Porch,' a website devoted to *Faking It*, and she will be answering all reader mail. Every letter will be answered, and readers with questions can be assured..."

"Well, I'll be," Zane said, astonished. "She's turning it all over to Denise."

"She isn't going to write a follow-up to *Faking It*?" Hunter chuckled. "This is the first time I've ever seen a bestselling author dump her fame into someone else's lap and take a hike."

Onscreen, Georgeanne listed Denise's qualifications and said, "No, Glen, I'm afraid I have nothing further to say about *Faking It*. But Denise has been hard at work for weeks, planning a sequel and answering reader mail. Believe me, no one is more qualified or better able to fill Fritzi Field's shoes."

"She's quitting." Zane still couldn't believe it.

"You didn't know about this?" Hunter asked.

"I've only talked to Georgie twice since she left." Zane frowned at the memory. "I was tempted to tell her to come back home, but she owes her readers something."

"Looks like she's taken care of that end on her own." Hunter got to his feet. "I'll go make coffee. So why haven't you called her more often?"

"Georgie deserves a chance to reap the benefits of her hard work," Zane said, wondering why the words left him feeling so hollow. "I don't want to influence her unfairly."

Hunter halted at the door to the kitchen. "So while you're busy being noble, the woman you want is getting the idea that you don't care about her?"

Zane gazed at Georgeanne, who looked a little thinner than he liked. "She can't possibly think that. I told her we needed to put our relationship on hold, and that we'd talk about us later." He watched Georgeanne's face, noting her practiced words and expression even as he remembered how hard he'd had to argue in order to get Georgeanne to see her duty. "It was the hardest thing I've ever done, but she deserves a chance to enjoy her success."

Hunter lounged against the doorframe. "For what it's worth, brother, poor old Georgie doesn't look particularly happy to me."

Chapter 12

Georgeanne lay on the bed in a Las Vegas hotel suite, which was exactly like the hotel suites she'd recently left in New York, Atlanta, Chicago, and Los Angeles, among other cities and stared at the television screen. It was one o'clock in the morning, and Georgeanne couldn't sleep.

"Our guests today are Miss Georgeanne Hartfield, also known as Fritzi Field, author of the best-selling book, *Faking It*, and the official Fritzi Field spokeswoman, Denise Devereaux," the hostess said. "Ms. Hartfield, Ms. Devereaux, welcome to 'Late Las Vegas Lights'."

The camera focused on Georgeanne's face while she politely thanked the hostess. Georgeanne realized that no amount of exposure would ever make her like seeing herself on television.

Worse, she had lost nearly fifteen pounds during the past four weeks. Even Georgeanne had to admit that she was probably the only woman in the United States whom weight loss didn't benefit.

Small wonder she had lost weight. She had toured the country and appeared on a grand total of sixty-four radio and television talk shows, sometimes doing four or five shows a day. She had autographed what seemed like sixty-four-thousand books, and she had spoken to what seemed like sixty-four-million fans.

Zane had been right, she realized. She did owe her readers this chance to see and hear her. He was also right in saying she was a writer, something she had never fully realized. She thought she had just gotten lucky. Thanks to Zane, she now knew that although a bestselling book might indeed be a lucky break, it was also the result of doing a lot of things right, and that *Faking It* was a book that Georgeanne Hartfield had been uniquely qualified to write.

Unfortunately, the only thing Georgeanne wished she had done right was tell Zane immediately that she was Fritzi Field. If she had, then maybe she wouldn't have fallen in love with him. Maybe she wouldn't have to face the American reading public with a stiff little smile and a heart that felt frozen.

"I remained anonymous because I was so ashamed of my own failure as a wife," she heard her television image say. "The book was an attempt to find a solution to that failure."

That was another thing Zane had been right about. She had nothing to be ashamed of. She had spoken for every woman in a situation similar to hers, and she had obviously hit quite a large target. And she offered a solution, for what it was worth. Not every woman was in a position to end her marriage and go in search of "Mr. Right."

Georgeanne watched herself turn the discussion over to Denise, who took over talking about *Faking It* while holding the book so the viewers could get a good view of the front cover. Denise defended the book to a couple of male hecklers in the audience with considerable verve and smilingly accepted the accolades of several loyal female fans.

Denise handled the discussion with aplomb, and Georgeanne sighed with relief. She had now appeared on a grand total of five talk shows with Denise beside her, and Georgeanne had seen immediately that Denise had what it took to send *Faking It* even higher on the bestseller lists. She exuded enthusiasm and dedication, and no question asked could throw her. Moreover, Denise had made vast inroads into the two boxes of Fritzi Field's letters, besides answering questions and posting essays daily on the official Fritzi Field website.

Denise, for all practical purposes, had become Fritzi Field. She probably knew as much about the book as its author, and she had already put together an outline for a sequel. Georgeanne had promised to help with the writing, but the ideas this time belonged to Denise, and Denise would be the one defending them publicly.

Thank God. She, Georgeanne, was going home. She wanted her old job back. She wanted to man her desk at the Saturday Clinic. She wanted her house and she wanted Roscoe and Jack beside her. She couldn't write without the proper surroundings and stimulation from people she liked.

She wanted Zane.

Sighing, Georgeanne turned the television off and flopped back down on the bed. Thank goodness she hadn't quit her job at the Gant Clinic. She could go home and take up her life again.

She'd see Zane on occasional Saturdays when he did his stint at the Saturday Clinic, and he needn't worry that she would embarrass him. She had plenty to do. But at least she could see him. That was better than not seeing him.

True, Zane had not officially ended their relationship, but she had figured that when he encouraged her to do the book tour, he was taking the polite way out, now that he knew she was Fritzi Field. She had hardly heard from him since.

Georgeanne frowned over the memory. At the time, she had believed him when he said he was proud of her. She hadn't realized the truth until she was a week into the tour, when she suddenly remembered his intense arguments about her duty to her readers. He was taking the least hurtful way of ending their relationship before it really got started.

Someone knocked at her door. She peered through the peephole then unlatched the door so Denise could enter.

"What are you doing still up?" she asked. "You're supposed to be up at five in the morning for the next show."

"I know. I'm too excited, I guess. I've been answering more of Fritzi's letters." She studied her friend. "Are you sure you want to quit the tour like this? We're selling books like crazy, and like it or not, you're still the real Fritzi Field."

"No, I'm not." Georgeanne was positive on that point. "You've taken on the job, so that makes you the real Fritzi Field as of right now. The truth is I have to have my dogs and my house and lots of peace and quiet in order to write. So if you want help with that sequel, your job is to keep the reporters and talk show hosts happy while I get the writing started."

"That's why I'm here." Denise clutched a sheaf of papers. "These are the ideas that came to me while I was answering questions this evening." She waved the papers at Georgeanne. "We may have to do two or three sequels, Georgie. It's unbelievable what the readers are telling me. They're writing the books for us."

Georgeanne smiled and agreed.

It was two o'clock by the time Denise wound down a little and returned to her own room. Georgeanne immediately returned to thinking about Zane.

She wondered what he would think when he turned up at the Saturday Clinic in a week or two and found her sitting at the front desk. Or what he would think if she visited him at his clinic under some pretext or other. More to the point, could she interest him in taking up where he left off?

She probably couldn't, Georgeanne's incurably honest alter ego answered. He had intimated that her career as a writer had taken off, and her duty was to nurture it. He seemed to think that a career as a famous writer was her life's dream or something.

Which was ridiculous. She liked writing, but she hated being famous and having everybody ask her things, as if she was some sort of know-it-all oracle. She wasn't cut out for doing talk shows and publicity tours, especially when they focused all eyes on her.

It was one thing to sit in her own home and write intimate advice to a nebulous but carefully targeted audience. It was quite another to advise a member of that audience in person. She was definitely not cut out to be a clinical psychologist, and she had been right to realize it before she signed up for courses.

She was destined to be a clinic receptionist and volunteer who wrote as a hobby about whatever interested her. Why couldn't Zane see that?

Georgeanne covered her face with her hands. She would have sworn Zane wanted her as much as she wanted him. She recalled him telling her they were involved in a serious relationship and heaved a deep sigh. He had meant it at the time. She knew he had.

So why had Zane practically pushed her onto an airplane to begin her book tour if he really wanted their relationship to prosper?

Unless he believed she had been faking her sexual response to him, once he discovered she had written *Faking It*.

Now that she thought about it, he had sounded almost angry when he told her what she owed her readers. The very idea was a stab to her heart. Surely it wasn't true.

Georgeanne had no answers to the questions circling in her brain, but she did know one thing. When she got home, she was driving to Houston. She would not return home until she knew, once and for all, exactly where she stood with Zane Bryant.

They had experienced wonderful sex together, something she had believed herself incapable of. He had shown her a whole new life, then he had taken it away. He owed her an explanation, by God, and she was going to get it.

Another knock sounded on her door. Georgeanne looked at the clock. Three o'clock in the morning. Denise was going to be a zombie on that early-morning talk show.

She went to the peephole, and gasped with astonishment when she saw Hunter Howell's handsome form through the tiny lens. She grabbed her robe off the bed and belted it securely before opening the door. If he intended to give her some sort of stay-away message from Zane, she wasn't sure what she'd do.

"About time," he said.

Georgeanne felt as if someone had thrown her off a cliff. "Zane? Why are you trying to look like your brother?"

Zane threw back his head and laughed. "I told him you'd recognize me right off. He seemed to think I should snow you for a few minutes." He forked his fingers through his hair and it fell back to its usual style. "Hunt's been reading too many movie scripts."

"Why did he think it would be a good thing for me to think you were him?" Georgeanne felt winded and dizzy. No doubt she was suffering heart palpitations on top of that, because she couldn't seem to think. "Or am I supposed to think he's you?"

Zane came inside and waited while she locked the door. "To tell you the truth, I'm not sure what he thought, but he's trying to be helpful. Georgie, you've lost entirely too much weight. Do you mind telling me what you think you're doing?"

"What I think I'm doing?" she echoed, baffled. "I've been doing this book tour you talked me into. But Denise is taking over for me, and I'm going home. Denise does Fritzi Field a lot better than I do. She's already planning a sequel, and talk show hosts love her personality. So I'm quitting with a good conscience. Why? Is that what you're afraid of?" she demanded.

"You're not making any sense." Zane frowned. "You're probably not thinking well due to an overall lack of nutrition. I'm ordering you a good meal from room service, and you're going to eat it."

"My thinking is perfectly clear, thank you." Georgeanne drew herself up and frowned back. "And I'm making sense, but you're not. What are you doing here, Zane? Did you come just to tell me I've lost too much weight, after you practically shoved me out the door for this tour?"

Her heart pounded so hard, Georgeanne noticed that she really was having trouble formulating thoughts. She wasn't making any sense to herself, and she trembled all over now that Zane was here.

Oh, she was a mental wreck, and in another minute, she was going to fling herself into his arms, whether he liked it or not.

The way he frowned, she very much feared he wouldn't like it.

"What do you mean shoved you out the door?" His intense stare seemed to look straight through her. "I did no such thing, other than tell you what your agent had been saying for weeks, that you owed your readers more than what you were giving them."

"I still say the book stands on its own. I have nothing more to add to it." Georgeanne struggled with an urge to bean him with the nearest object. "If you're here because you think I was putting Fritzi Field's advice into practice when I slept with you, then you'd better leave now before I beat you to death with a pillow."

His frown vanished into astonishment. "You think I thought you were faking your sexual response with me?"

"Well, what else am I supposed to think?" Georgeanne said, her voice rising. "The minute you found out I was Fritzi Field, you couldn't get rid of me fast enough. But that's beside the point. The point is, why are you here now?"

"I came to grab you by the hair and drag you home, of course." He folded his arms across his chest. "Are you going to come peacefully, or do I have to do the caveman act?"

Georgeanne drew in air and told herself she could not possibly be hearing correctly. "Have you been taking acting lessons from Hunter about how to be a caveman?"

"I don't need lessons." Zane unfolded his arms and came toward her with purpose in every motion. "I do a great caveman act."

Georgeanne took a few steps back and watched him approach with wide eyes as an impossible joy swept through her. "In that case, maybe I'm the one who needs lessons."

He stopped in front of her and took her shoulders in his hands. "Georgie, I've missed you so much. Now I'm going to take up right where we left off over a month ago."

"I thought—I was afraid you wouldn't want to." Georgeanne watched his big fingers untie the knot in her robe and almost trembled with a powerful mix of joy and desire.

"Why on earth not?" Zane slid his hands up to push the robe off her shoulders. "You're mine. I've been wanting to kill every male talk show host who hugged up to you."

"I hate talk shows." She did tremble when he ran his hands down the sides of the silky nightgown she wore. "I was coming to your apartment as soon as I got home."

"Were you." He smiled at her. "What for?"

"To have it out with you, of course." Georgeanne, filled with joyful disbelief, laughed breathlessly. "I hate book tours, Zane, but you were right. It was something I owed my publisher and agent, and my readers. It's over now, and I'm not going on another one. I've hired a personal representative to take care of all that for me."

"Denise?" He ran his hands over her rib cage.

"Denise loves being Fritzi Field."

"Are you sure, Georgie?" Zane asked.

She pushed back slightly and looked at him. "I was never more sure of anything in my life. It...occurred to me that maybe you thought...that maybe you thought I liked book tours and being a well-known author. So I decided that when I got home, I'd better come tell you how I really feel about it."

"So how do you really feel about being a famous author?"

Georgeanne sought for words. It wasn't easy when Zane gently drew her nightgown off over her head. "An author's job is to write books, but when a book is as successful as *Faking It*, readers expect and deserve a lot more." She stopped and swallowed hard. "I wanted to thank you for pointing that out to me. You were right when you said I had a responsibility to my readers."

Zane nodded and tossed her nightgown aside. "Go on, please."

"But before I left, I had already learned something else, something even more important. I learned that there really is one man for every woman, a man who can make her feel all the things people talk about and poets write poems about." In fact, she wanted to add, she was feeling some of them now.

"Mr. Right?" Zane asked, staring at her breasts.

"Yes." Georgeanne found that everything inside her responded to his glittering, intent expression. For a writer, she wasn't exactly flowing with glowing prose just now when she needed it most. "Zane, I'm trying to tell you that I love you. And that I would never have left home if you hadn't showed me what I owed my readers."

Zane dragged Georgeanne into his arms. "Thank God. I thought you never were going to say it. Georgie, I love you. I think I've loved you since you wrote me that first letter about the Saturday Clinic. I was afraid that you'd lose interest in me as soon as you realized you had a successful career as Fritzi Field."

"Never." She rode in his arms to the bed, glorying in his strength and the fact that he loved her. "What's a career compared to you?"

"I was afraid to find out the answer to that." He laid her in the center of the bed and stepped back to shed his own clothing without taking his eyes from her. "I knew there wasn't much I could do to advance your writing career, even if I became a cardiologist."

"You'd be wasted as a cardiologist." Georgeanne could barely speak when he bared himself to her view. "Besides, you'd probably be personally responsible for a lot of female cardiac deaths." She gave him a tremulous smile. "It would be irresponsible of me to let you become a heart doctor."

"Good, because I would be equally irresponsible if I let you do any more talk shows." He came to her, all rugged masculinity, and took her in his arms. "I'm surprised those talk show hosts aren't getting calls from men who want to meet you."

"So they can show me what Fritzi Field is missing?" Georgeanne couldn't help herself and began to laugh softly. "They've gotten dozens of calls, and each of the male callers thinks he'll be the one who can turn Fritzi Field into a real woman."

"What?" Zane sounded outraged. "That does it. You're through with talk shows, Georgie Hartfield."

"That's what I've been trying to tell you." She smiled up at him as he leaned over her. "Denise makes pancakes out of anyone who tries to come on to her or harass her. Talk show hosts love her. She creates the kind of controversy they adore."

Zane gazed at Georgeanne's breasts and cupped one in his palm. "Good. I have a feeling Denise is going to shine as Fritzi Field. I'll bet she's having a great time."

His mouth replaced his palm, and Georgeanne drew in a quivering breath. "She is, but not nearly as much as I'm enjoying the process of being turned into a real woman."

• • •

Three months later, Georgeanne awakened early one morning to find Zane beside her with a tray in his hands. He set the tray on the bedside stand and she saw that it carried a hearty breakfast of eggs, bacon, and oatmeal, a vase that held a single rose, and a cup of fragrant coffee.

"Wake up, Mrs. Bryant," Zane said. "The world awaits."

She stretched and yawned, conscious of his appreciative gaze. "That's one thing nobody ever told me. Doctors have the ability to leap out of bed, fully awake and aware at an unearthly hour of the morning."

"We learn it in residency." Zane sat on the edge of the bed beside her. "You have to go from deep sleep to full diagnostic mode inside of two minutes. I have something to tell you as soon as you've had a few sips of coffee."

"Oh?" Georgeanne sat up and stacked pillows behind her. "Does this have anything to do with my new book idea by any chance?"

"As a matter of fact, it does." Zane stroked her tumbled hair back from her face. "Dr. Baghri wants you to accept a new position at the Saturday Clinic."

"I don't know about that, Zane." She studied his face, amazed at the strength of the emotions just the sight of him evoked. "The only position I understand at the Saturday Clinic is the front desk. I don't have any medical training whatsoever."

"He wants you to take the position of Director. He says it's the only way to make sure you keep doing everything you've been doing." He grinned at her expression as he transferred the breakfast tray to her lap. "I think he's afraid you're going to write another bestselling book and take off on another book tour. The Saturday Clinic nearly collapsed under the weight of patients while you were gone."

"That's the least of his worries." Georgeanne nibbled a piece of crisp bacon. "I finished my outline last night. Telling the story of the Saturday Clinic might get other clinics started all over the country. Plus, it's the only way I can memorialize what brought us together."

"And Dr. Baghri is the one who'll have to do the book tours?" Zane outlined her lips with one finger. "That's an excellent idea, because that brings me to my next piece of news. I've decided to join the Gant Clinic two days a week—the two days Dr. Baghri will be taking off to help start Saturday Clinics in other areas of the country."

"I'm glad, Zane," Georgeanne said. "It worries me, making you drive almost an hour every morning and evening, when we could have just moved into your apartment."

"Not likely, when we have this house in the country. I wanted to live here with you since the first day I saw the place. Not to mention the fact that Roscoe and Jack probably wouldn't adapt very well to life in the city." He watched her spoon up oatmeal with close attention.

"The dogs wouldn't know how to act in an apartment," she agreed dryly.

"And I wouldn't want you to be the one on the road twice a day, so don't even think about it," Zane said. "I'm going to maintain an office here and one in Pasadena for the next few years. Eventually, I'll close the office in Pasadena and move my practice here. I've decided I like country living." He watched her lips as she sipped coffee. "So what are you doing today?"

Georgeanne moved the tray off her lap and put her arms around his neck. "I'm going to work, of course. Then I'm coming home and cooking a special dinner for you."

"In that case, I'll try to get home early." He looked into her eyes and gave her a smoldering smile. "Maybe you can model that new yellow bikini for me."

"I'll wear anything you want, Zane," she promised, smiling. "But I can't promise I won't blush while I'm wearing it. It's really tiny."

"I've missed seeing you blush. Since Denise has taken over as Fritzi Field, your complexion has stayed on an even keel."

Georgeanne laughed softly. "In that case, I'll add some fancy dancing to the display of the bikini. I can guarantee you'll see plenty of blushing."

"I can't wait."

Neither could she. Still amazed at her own thoughts, Georgeanne laid her open palms on Zane's shoulders. She almost felt she owed the world a follow-up book entitled something along the lines of *Finding Mr. Right*, but what could she say that hadn't already been said?

Unless, of course, she decided to title the book, *Love Means Never Having To Fake It Again*.

On second thought, Georgeanne decided as Zane sought her lips for a long, tender kiss, she would let well enough alone. Denise had already turned in an outline to Alice Anson for a follow-up to

Faking It, and Georgeanne had high hopes for her outline of *The Story of The Saturday Clinic*. She didn't have time to write a book on finding Mr. Right. It was enough that she had actually found him.

Zane sat back and studied her figure appreciatively. "You'd better eat all your breakfast or there won't be anything left of you to fill out a bikini."

Georgeanne's heart thrilled at the caring possessiveness in his voice, even though she had regained half of her lost fifteen pounds. "Are you saying I'm looking a mite peaked, Doctor?"

"Darned right I am." Zane touched her cheek. "In fact, you look like a woman who needs a doctor."

Georgeanne looked at him with her heart in her eyes. "Then it's a good thing I married one, isn't it?"

"The doctor is always in for you, Georgie."

She saw the same vision of the future shining in Zane's eyes that she hoped he saw in hers, a future of shared love and laughter.

Together, they were strong—strong enough to make a difference in other lives, because of the power of their love.

About the Author

Kathryn Brocato is a lifelong reader and writer of romance who lives with her husband, dogs, and chickens in Southeast Texas. Learn more about her at *www.kathrynbrocato.com*, and visit her Facebook page at *http://www.facebook.com/pages/ Kathryn-Brocato-Author/130436237088005.*

A Sneak Peek from Crimson Romance
(From *Passionfruit & Poetry* by Téa Cooper)

Jeanie Baker's fingers tightened on the tiny black apron with the frill of white lace. No way. Out of the question. Nothing this side of hell would make her wear it. It belonged in a French porn movie, not in Oldbridge. Not in a café serving coffee, cake and sympathy to the small rural community. Groping around her back she wrenched off the offending scrap of material, screwed it into a very tight ball, and flung it at the coffee machine.

"I'm not wearing it, Gran. Not for you, not for anyone." Expecting a complaint, she shot a sideways glance at her grandmother.

"But sweetheart, it suits the café. Our ambience. They are here to film, to take photographs, and they've come especially because of the style of the place."

Rolling her eyes, Jeanie laughed. "I'm not wearing it. And that's that. They'll just have to put up with me the way I am and besides you told me it was the location they were interested in and that's why they're here. Not to photograph us."

Sometimes Jeanie wished her grandmother could be just a little more ordinary, a little less out there. She loved the café with its quirky décor and old movie posters and was more than happy to help in anyway she could. After all, she certainly owed her grandmother more than she could ever repay, but she drew the line at making a spectacle of herself. She belonged in the background, taking care of the day to day running of the place not dressing up like some model, pretending to be something she knew she could never be.

"I suppose you're right, but I think you're ten times prettier than the motley crew out there." Norma peered out through the window of the Café Cinématique. "Emaciated, that's what they are."

Over the top of her grandmother's curly white hair, Jeanie stared at the odd assortment of bodies and vehicles spilling out across the footpath. People movers and four-wheel drives, cameras, and lighting filled every available space as far as she could see. All for a magazine shoot to showcase the latest range of outlandish city chic.

"Oh!" Norma's floury fingernail tapped the window and she turned. "There's the makeup crew and they're setting up shop across the road in front of the library. I bet poor old Wilma will be having a heart attack."

Within the space of half an hour, the empty street had filled and was crawling with activity, even busier than the days before they diverted the highway around the town. Unbelievable! Then again maybe this wasn't such a bad idea if it improved the café's turnover. It would be nice, just for once to be able to make the mortgage payments.

"Gran, I think I owe you an apology. I don't think your idea was a silly as it sounded."

"And which particular idea was that, my darling?" Norma's eyes twinkled as she turned around and Jeanie recognized the self-satisfied smile on her lined face.

"You know very well."

"Yes, but I like to hear it. It's not every day I get praise from my favorite granddaughter."

"Only granddaughter." Jeanie paused and stared straight into her familiar eyes. "It was a brilliant idea to list the café on the Locations-R-Us website. If we become a popular location it will mean more people coming into the café. You've put us on the map." Jeanie put her arm around her grandmother's shoulder and hugged her tight. "However, there's just one problem—I am categorically not dressing up like some French waitress from a seedy porn movie. Not for you. Not for the Café Cinématique. Not for anyone. They've got models to do that."

Norma's floury finger tapped Jeanie's nose and she screwed up her face and grinned as she waited for the next insight into the world according to Norma. "This might just be the beginning. Great trees from little apples grow. This might only be a fashion shoot, but the next one may be our movie contract, and we could be extras. Are you sure you don't want to wear the apron?"

Certain, absolutely certain.

In fact, the entire circus made Jeanie's stomach churn. She resisted the temptation to pull her grandmother into her arms and hug her. So much heart in such a little package, but it was unlikely it would make any permanent difference. The small town just couldn't support three cafés anymore. Even with Norma's magic baking touch, no one's fortune was going to be made from cakes and cups of coffee.

"Oh! There's someone coming in." Norma pulled away from the window and smoothed the black and white frilled apron over her sensible floral cotton dress.

The old bell on the top of the door danced on its metal bracket and the plastic strips over the doorway parted.

"Right, we're here, and here's the schedule for the day." A skimpily dressed waif with black eyes and lips to match waved an iPad under her grandmother's nose. "I'm Jaz. I emailed you a copy, but there have been a few changes since then and we need to make sure you have locked them in."

Jeanie registered the panic flicker in her grandmother's eyes.

Email. Her department.

Jeanie hadn't bothered to print the wretched schedule; just ignored it hoping the horror wouldn't eventuate. Her stomach sank. Or had she trashed it?

"Perhaps you could email me the update." She tilted the corners of her mouth, using the very special smile she reserved for the Country Women's Association ladies when they were arguing about jam. Amazingly, it seemed to work. The waif's black nails tipped and tapped.

"You got it." Jaz turned on her elegantly unlaced Converse sneakers and, holding the door open, issued another gem. "Mr. Fitzgerald likes to do his own shoot preview and he likes his coffee short, black, and strong. And a skinny soy latte for me. Then you better go outside and get the coffee orders from the girls and take bottled water. They need water, lots of it."

Her black tipped fingers waved randomly at the glass-door fridges and then she disappeared in a fluttering storm of plastic strips. It was going to be a long day.

With her arms crossed and her foot tapping, Jeanie let out a long slow breath and shot a look at her grandmother. Norma's penciled eyebrows danced back at her. "I reckon she could do with a decent feed—low blood sugar plays havoc with my temper too. I'll get the coffee machine started."

Jeanie smothered a laugh. "And I'll print the email. Then at least we know what to expect and when."

Turning sideways, she eased her way past the big chest freezer and boxes of soft drinks stacked haphazardly in the passageway and squeezed into the tiny cubbyhole where the battered PC sat like an expectant toad next to a bundle of white fluff. A few lights flickered in a half-hearted fashion.

"Come on, Coco." The dog vacated the table and leaped straight into her lap. Running her fingers absently through the silky ears, Jeanie peered at the screen, waiting for the email to show up. She didn't want to spoil her grandmother's latest moneymaking scheme—she just wanted the whole event to be worth the upheaval. The unchanging weekly routine of her life suited her; knowing where she stood and what to expect gave her a sense of security and peace. But the café did need an injection of cash if it was going to stay afloat.

Most of the regular events Jeanie had been able to reschedule. The Crafty Yarns group had agreed to change their day but it meant they'd clash with Pencil Orchids tomorrow, and they wouldn't like that. The writing group insisted on peace and quiet so everyone could hear their poetry readings and the Crafty Yarners wanted to gossip and spin tales.

She shook her head, pulled up the email, and hit print. The ancient printer coughed, spluttered, and groaned before finally co-operating and producing a slightly smudged version of the day's schedule.

"Okay, Coco. Let's go." She settled the dog back on the cushioned plastic seat then reefed the sheet of paper from the printer.

• • •

A soprano laugh tinkled down the passageway followed by a deep baritone. Jeanie slowed and sneaked a peek around the fridges. Her grandmother had obviously found her cameraman.

Hands clasped under her chin, Norma stared up adoringly into the eyes of a tall man who stood casually at the counter, fork hovering near his perfect white teeth as he sampled the piece of lemon pie. He positively towered over her grandmother. The two massive cameras slung over his broad shoulder might as well have been matchbox toys.

"Oh, Mr. Fitzgerald, thank you," Norma cooed, her eyelashes making the ceiling fans redundant. "I'm so glad you like it."

Jeanie blinked. Even she'd heard of Xander Fitzgerald, fashion photographer to the rich and famous. Only a few weeks ago, she'd read an article about him in one of the Sunday magazines. Judging by the two hefty cameras, and the fact that Norma had called him by name, it had to be the renowned photographer making her grandmother go weak at the knees while he sampled her culinary delights.

Looking every bit as good as any of Gran's poster pinups, Xander Fitzgerald walked along the length of the counter carrying his plate of lemon and passionfruit pie with him. He pointed with his fork to each of the movie posters adorning the walls, reading aloud the names of the movies and the stars in a deep voice that made Jeanie think of the last bit of chocolate at the bottom of a milkshake. Then he turned, licked his lips, and put the plate on the counter, gazing down at her grandmother.

"Frankly, my dear, I *do* give a damn—this is about the best lemon pie I have ever tasted."

Jeanie grimaced. Corny. So bad. It was a good job her grandmother was well over the age of consent. She could see her arthritic knees going weak. Time to intervene and get the show on the road. The sooner the photo shoot finished the sooner her life could return to normal.

She studied the piece of paper in her hand.

7 to 7:15: shoot preview.

Presumably that's what was happening now. Time to make a move.

With a steadying breath, she walked up, hand outstretched and a tight smile plastered on her face. "Good morning, Mr. Fitzgerald."

He turned and a gasp of surprise froze in Jeanie's throat. Colored contacts. It had to be—his eyes were exactly the same navy as his shirt. Definitely contacts. Somehow her hand ended up in his—she glanced down at it and something jumped inside her, then she jerked her hand back as he started to speak.

"Good morning, you must be Jeanie. Your grandmother was just telling me about the lovely little business she's been running here for longer than I can believe."

Forcing her lips back into a smile Jeanie studied the navy-eyed smooth talker, trying to ignore the coy titters emanating from the direction of her grandmother.

On closer inspection he wasn't as young as she'd thought, which was probably why Gran was making such a fool of herself. Once a man turned thirty, he was fair game in Gran's book—any younger and she deemed it cradle snatching.

Fine lines radiated out from the corners of his eyes and the non-designer stubble on his chin gave him an almost negligent air, as though he'd been in a bit of a hurry to leave the house, and the creased linen shirt only added to it.

She cleared her throat and beat down the flush on her cheeks. "We don't get many complaints. Gran's the talented one. I just make the coffee and clear the tables."

His vivid gaze roamed backward and forward across her face and a shot of something as potent as the brandy Gran put in her Christmas cakes raced through her. Her toes tingled. She lifted her hand to her face and brushed her hair away from her forehead. Perhaps they'd need the fans on with all these extra people around. It was very warm in the café.

"Have we met before?" he asked.

In the mood for more Crimson Romance?
Check out *Lost Without You*
by Heather Thurmeier
at *CrimsonRomance.com*.